PULP LITERATURE PRESS

Issue No. 44, Autumn 2024

Publisher: Pulp Literature Press; Editor-in-Chief: Jennifer Landels; Senior Editor: Mel Anastasiou; Acquisitions Editor: Genevieve Wynand; Poetry Editors: Daniel Cowper & Emily Osborne; Copy Editor: Amanda Bidnall; Russian Editor: Anna Belkine; Proofreader: Sierra Louie; Graphic Design: Amanda Bidnall & Sierra Louie; Cover Design: Kate Landels; Subscriptions: Carol McCauley; First Readers: Amber Allen, Mark Cameron, Michaela Chan, Summer Keown, Sylvia Leong, Tara Smalldon. For advertising rates, direct inquiries to info@pulpliterature.com.

Cover painting, *Ceren of the Surf* by Bronwyn Schuster. Illustrations for 'Bad Backup' by Gabriel Craven and Mikayla Fawcett. All other illustrations by Mel Anastasiou.

Pulp Literature: ISSN 2292-2164 (Print), ISSN 2292-2172 (Digital), Issue No. 44, Autumn 2024.

Published quarterly by Pulp Literature Press, 21955 16 Ave, Langley, BC, Canada V2Z 1K5, pulpliterature.com, at $18.00 per copy. Annual subscription $60.00 in Canada, $80.00 in continental USA, $92.00 elsewhere. Printed in Surrey, BC, Canada, by Fraser Printers Ltd. Copyright © 2024 Pulp Literature Press. All stories and works of art copyright © 2024 their authors as per bylines.

Pulp Literature Press is based in the unceded traditional Coast Salish Territories of the Katzie, Kwantlen, Matsqui, and Semiahmoo First Nations.

Pulp Literature Press gratefully acknowledges the support of the Canada Council for the Arts and the Government of Canada.

Pulp Literature is a proud member of the Magazine Association of BC and Magazines Canada.

TABLE OF CONTENTS

FROM THE PULP LIT PULPIT

Begin Again

For the past five years, I have had the great joy of presiding over the pages of the Pulp Lit Pulpit. This will be my seventeenth—and final—editorial for the magazine. In my first, I shared the oft-quoted line *to every thing there is a season, and a time to every purpose*. It felt so easy then to imagine the beginning of something grand. It feels quite melancholy now to acknowledge its end.

In preparing to write this editorial, I re-read its predecessors. As with most ongoing narratives, some themes emerged, the four seasons chief among them. Cyclical chapters of a larger story, the seasons remind us that we too can be our very own alchemists of change. Beginnings lead to endings lead to beginnings. And autumn, in all its gold and burgundy and pumpkin-spiced glory, offers up the year's final acts of beauty before we are asked—no, told—to let go of it all.

Eventually and always, the present belongs to the past. This isn't the makings of a koan; it is simply the beating heart of Time. We feel its rhythm all around us. In the changing seasons, yes, but also in fashion and technology and language. We see it in the ageing face of a loved one. In the stories within these pages.

I've heard it said that we need not mourn an ending, for there is, in fact, no such thing as an ending—only the place you choose to stop a story. But to me, if something has mattered, the finishing of that thing is always at least a little bit sad. Even when you are excited about all that is to come.

Although I am stepping away from the editorial dais, I look forward to settling into a comfy chair and joining you, dear *Pulp Literature* readers. I can't wait to see all the once-upon-a-times and happily-ever-afters (or not!) still to come. Thank you for the seasons we have shared.

~Genevieve Wynand

In THIS ISSUE

Ceren of the Surf, one of cover artist **Bronwyn Schuster**'s Knights of the Drowned Table, guards the watery portal to our autumn offerings. But more than water flows past the dead in feature author **Kate Heartfield**'s chilling tale of corporate cover-ups, 'The Investigation Is Sealed'.

Ravens, monsters, and zombies steal the show—and a few souls—in 'A Fair Exchange' by **Tom Jolly**, 'Liar's Leap' by **Jonathan Sean Lyster**, and 'Bad Backup' by **Mikayla Fawcett** and **Gabriel Craven**.

Meanwhile, artistic adventures in celluloid and spider's silk await in 'The Projectionist' by **Lisa Alo Seaman** and 'A Weaver's Web' by **Barry Charman.**

The smell of goats and the secrets of ghosts haunt the pages of 'The Shepherdess: Narbonne' by **JM Landels** and 'Take My Hand: Enter Night' by **Mel Anastasiou.**

And poetry from our Magpie Award winners **Angela Rebrec, Cicely Grace,** and **Veronika Gorlova** reminds us that even the darkest of nights end in sunrise.

THE INVESTIGATION IS SEALED

Kate Heartfield

Kate Heartfield's novels include The Valkyrie, The Embroidered Book, and The Chatelaine. She has won the Aurora Award for Best Novel three times. Her fiction has been shortlisted for the World Fantasy, Nebula, Locus, Sunburst, and Crawford awards, as well as the Ottawa Book Award, and her journalism has been shortlisted for a National Newspaper Award. Kate's story 'And in the Arcade, Ego' was featured in Issue 33, Winter 2022. 'The Investigation Is Sealed' is very loosely inspired by the Westray mine disaster of 1992 and the song about it by the Canadian band Weeping Tile. Kate grew up in Manitoba and now lives in Ottawa. Visit her at kateheartfield.com.

The Investigation Is Sealed

The draeger flowed into the mine shaft like thin, pale honey. At the entrance, the chief alchemical investigator supervised the application, though his job was mostly done. He'd made the stuff. He'd poured it onto the ground, just inside the blown-apart doors. There was little to do now but watch it grow, from a pint to many gallons, feeding on disaster.

"What happens next?" asked the chief of police, standing and watching in the way men in uniform stand and watch.

"Stand well back, please. Once it reaches the end, I can take a sample and analyze the changes."

"And it will tell you … what happened? Whether there's …"

The chief alchemical investigator breathed in rotten, burnt air. There was no way any miners within would be alive. He needed no potion to tell him that, though the draeger was, as always, eager to tell him. It was a powerful potion, and it spoke to its maker. When he squatted casually and dampened his fingers, he saw flashes of what the draeger found.

Shining and clear it flowed, with canary-yellow glints near the doors where the weak morning sun hit. It dampened the layer of coal dust that lay unburned near the entrance—the remnants of the stuff that had acted like gunpowder when the coal seam breathed methane onto some unknown spark. The golden liquid flowed an inch deep, in the opposite direction the fireball had taken. It flowed past twisted equipment, seeping into a charred body trapped beneath it: the body of a man who'd told his supervisor about dangerous amounts of coal dust.

"Any investigating potion can tell us a lot," said the chief alchemical investigator, standing up again, resisting the urge to wipe his wet fingertips on his pants. "Draeger absorbs truth the way analyn absorbs pain, the way eljanbar absorbs pressure, or the way some alchemists hoped mirasol would absorb energy. The truth of what happened here will be in the draeger."

Footsteps behind them, and they turned to see the chief executive officer in a dark suit. She gave them a professional nod of acknowledgement. They were all in this together. Government, police, the company, the mining alchemists, and the town full of miners and their families, who needed work to live, just as everyone did. This was not an economy that could weather a corporate collapse.

"We're all eager to get to the bottom of this," said the chief executive officer. "It's such a privilege to be a part of a company that's not afraid of the truth. There's a reason there has never been a prosecution at any of our mines."

The chief alchemical investigator agreed. His fingertips stung. The ground shuddered, and the police officers, standing at a safe distance behind the barrier, looked nervous. But this was no explosion. What they felt was the draeger reaching the end of the mine.

When it could flow no further, it deepened. Two inches thick, then three. Covering the bodies that lay scattered, and the ones under the rock fall, and the ones that were no longer whole.

It learned their names and stories as it filled their open mouths and glazed their staring eyes.

It filled the mine shafts to the top. It drowned the wrenched tracks and blackened signs.

And when it had filled the mine, it hardened like amber and darkened like blood. At the broken threshold, there was now a wall, nearly as opaque as dirt.

It knew how and why every one of those miners died. It knew about the woman who'd reported the sparking conveyor. It had fed on and absorbed the truth until there was no truth left for anyone to learn. Truth lived now only in the draeger, congealing in the air that no longer smelled like death.

Now the families in the little houses a mile away would have nothing to grieve, only absences that hurt too much to examine or explain. Everyone would forget.

Everyone but the chief alchemical investigator, whose fingertips still felt damp.

He didn't shake the hand of the chief executive officer when she held it out.

"Excellent work," she said, brightly. "The whole company will be glad to have it confirmed that the mine was empty. Our employee family can be confident in a safety record that remains unblemished."

Another tomb locked into the mind of the chief alchemical investigator. This was the only choice he made: to always touch the draeger, so that someone would remember. But he kept his silence. He had a little house in another little town, with a family in it. He knew his job and his place.

He opened his dry lips and said, "I pronounce this investigation sealed."

FEATURE INTERVIEW

Kate Heartfield

Pulp Literature: *You say in your bio that this chilling story is loosely based on the Westray Mine disaster. Can you tell us a bit more about it, and why you wanted to write about it?*

Kate Heartfield: It was a coal mine in Nova Scotia which closed less than a year after it opened when a terrible explosion in May 1992 killed 26 miners. Eleven of them are still entombed in the mine, as their bodies were not able to be recovered, and I hope this story honours them and their colleagues in some small way. A public inquiry found that the explosion was caused by "a complex mosaic of actions, omissions, mistakes, incompetence, apathy, cynicism, stupidity and neglect" but there was never full accountability for those in charge. The disaster happened when I was in high school in Manitoba and I remember reading the news stories at the time. To me, it's a story that exposes how much of our corporate system rests on violence and untruths and sees human lives as disposable. One day in 2022, nearly 30 years after the explosion, I was brainstorming ideas for a flash fiction contest for the Codex writers group. I was using two prompts: one of them was to find a sentence on page 26 of a nearby book. That sentence had the word 'investigation' in it. I had been listening to the song about Westray by the band

Weeping Tile, and my thoughts returned to the disaster. Another of the prompts was to write about a liquid with unusual properties. The word 'draeger' in the story is inspired by 'draegermen', a word for mine rescuers.

PL: *Many of your novels are historical fantasy. What draws you to write about the past through the lens of magic? When a story idea comes to you, what comes first, the magic or the history?*

Kate Heartfield: I find the past inherently uncanny, because it feels so familiar—we recognize places and we see the connections to our own lives, and yet it's another world, one we can never visit and one that we struggle to understand. We see it through a glass darkly, and we speculate on it. That's not very different from speculating in other ways. Adding magic to historical fiction is a way of spinning the lens of the kaleidoscope, of showing the apparently familiar in a new light. It keeps the reader on the back foot, not sure of what is possible in this version of history, which can be a very useful tool for a storyteller. As for which comes first, it depends on the story, but often I am literalizing a metaphor—as in this story. I frequently draw the fantastical elements from the same sources as the historical ones, so that the magic in the story feels of a piece with the rest. For example, in my novel *The Valkyrie*, I was drawing on old tales that included historical elements such as Atilla the Hun and fantastical elements such as dragons, so it only made sense for my version to do the same.

PL: *We hear you wield a longsword in your spare time. Does putting historical steel in your hands help translate history to the page?*

Kate Heartfield: I've been taking longsword classes and workshops here in Ottawa for about a year, in addition to a shorter stint I did before the pandemic. It's a lot of fun and it's really good for my overall health to do something that uses my body and brain in a different way after I've been sitting at my computer all day. It's also great for research, of course. Even though I'm extremely novice and I have a lot to learn, I do think that getting to grips (so to speak) with the physical processes you're writing about can be helpful for a writer, and swords or other bladed weapons do tend to make appearances in historical fantasy. Whenever I can draw on the actual experience of doing something in more or less the same way it would have been done generations ago, whether it's rowing a boat, shooting an arrow, embroidering a cushion, or baking bread, I find that really valuable, and I also love the connection across time, as so many of those activities haven't changed much.

PL: *Can you tell us a bit about your writing process? Are you a pantser or a plotter, a disciplined nine-to-fiver or a victim of the whims of your muse?*

Kate Heartfield: I'm probably not as disciplined as I could be, but I tend to hit my deadlines, in part thanks to many years as a newspaper journalist. I do write synopses and outlines at the beginning of long projects, but I tend to deviate from my outlines a lot as I go, so I do a lot of revision. Short stories, such as 'The Investigation Is Sealed', don't usually require outlines. I might just jot a few words down to remind myself to hit certain beats or incorporate certain elements, but usually I can see the shape of a story that size well enough that I can just start writing. Novels, not so much!

PL: *What advice do you have for Canadian writers in today's publishing world?*

Kate Heartfield: Publishing can be an incredibly frustrating business, and every writer has a different (unpredictable) path. There are two things that have helped keep me from running off into the hills and never writing again. First, community. Having other writers who can listen to you vent, or cheer you on in the good times, is a huge help, and we are all stronger together. Second, I think there's a lot to be said for writing the strange stories of one's heart. There's a tension, there, of course, because art is outward-looking too and we are trying to communicate to people who are not ourselves. But the whole point of that communication is to connect with the deepest, wildest parts of ourselves, and so I think the temptation to water down our writing to make it more marketable is self-defeating. One thing I really appreciate about *Pulp Literature* is that it has given me space for stories that stretched my own limits as a writer, stories in which I'm trusting the reader to come along without a lot of exposition: this one, and a previous story, 'And in the Arcade, Ego'.

PL: *Congratulations on the Aurora Award hat trick for* The Valkyrie *(2024),* The Embroidered Book *(2023), and* The Chatelaine / Armed in Her Fashion *(2019). Is there another future award winner in the works?*

Kate Heartfield: Thank you! I was truly astonished to win the third Aurora this year, and it's a great honour, especially given the incredible books on the ballot. My next novel is *The Tapestry of Time,* out from HarperCollins in Canada on October 1, 2024.

It's about four clairvoyant sisters fighting Nazis for control of the Bayeux Tapestry in the summer of 1944. My next novel after that will be *Mercutio*, a prequel to Shakespeare's *Romeo and Juliet*, which I've nearly finished. And there are a couple of other things yet to be announced. So I'm keeping busy.

PL: *Thank you so much for your time. We can't wait to get our eyes on those new books!*

Select Bibliography

The Tapestry of Time, 2024 (HarperVoyager UK)
The Valkyrie, 2023 (HarperVoyager UK)
The Chatelaine, 2023 (HarperVoyager UK)
The Embroidered Book, 2022 (HarperVoyager UK)
The Magician's Workshop, 2019 (Choice of Games)
The Road to Canterbury, 2018 (Choice of Games)
Alice Payne Rides, 2019 (Tordotcom Publishing)
Alice Payne Arrives, 2018 (Tordotcom Publishing)
'The Course of True Love', in *Monstrous Little Voices: New Tales from Shakespeare's Fantasy World*, 2016 (Abaddon Books)

TAKE MY HAND: EXIT LIGHT

Mel Anastasiou

Mel Anastasiou writes the Fairmount Manor Mysteries, the Hertfordshire Pub Mysteries, and the Monument Studios Mysteries. Winner of a Literary Titan Gold award and longlisted for the Leacock Medal, Mel is also the author of two illustrated thirty-day workbooks on story structure: the steampunk-themed The Writer's Boon Companion and The Writer's Friend and Confidante. For news on published and upcoming works, visit her website, melanastasiou.wordpress.com.

Take My Hand
Part 2: Exit Light

It's April 1991. Jamie Stewart, a night orderly in a city hospital, is in the grip of a haunting that, in darkness, takes her over entirely. And in daytime she hides from the criminal family she escaped months before.

Chapter 9

Jamie cradled her aching right hand. On her lap lay the final page from the ghost's latest possession of her. More pages were stacked on her coffee table. Seconds before, the ghost had held her blind and immobile. Now he was gone.

She managed one free breath before she heard a clatter in the kitchen. Wes, who was meant to be waiting outside her apartment building in his Le Mans, sat down next to her on the sofa.

He said, "You're back. From concentrating. On your writing, I mean."

"How did you get into my place?"

"Door's unlocked. It was cooling down outside, so I brought my book in with me."

Jamie glanced down at *The Quick Red Fox* on the coffee table, half-hidden by the pages of the ghost's writing.

Wes continued, "We did have dinner plans. I thought you wouldn't mind if I waited here."

When Jamie didn't answer, Wes coloured. "Maybe I was wrong. Anyway, somebody named Zane was shouting at you on your machine to pick up, so I did. She said a patient named Maria got her tests back and you'd want to know before your early shift on Monday. They came out negative. It sounded like good news?"

Jamie nodded.

"I didn't know you were a nurse as well as a writer."

She said, "I'm an orderly."

She had nothing to add to this statement that wasn't an obfuscation or a lie. Already her deceptions divided her from Wes. She couldn't bear to tell him even one more untruth, but reality sounded like a lie. *I'm not a writer, I'm an orderly with a boring life, as beige as this sofa, except when I'm being possessed by a ghost. Or chased by a family of criminals.*

She put a hand to her forehead. Her head felt stretched, as if Casey had been moving around inside her brain like Dylan inside his ectoplasm; as if the teenager, the ghost, and she were a set of nesting dolls.

Wes said, "I've been kind of studying you while you write. Not creepily, though. Respectfully."

"You've been staring at me?"

He coloured. "Maybe I should have stayed downstairs in the car. It seemed all right at the time, but now? Maybe not. You can throw me out."

"We had a date, though. You must have thought I was standing you up."

"Actually, you should throw me out. Then I'd have to figure out how to win a girl back. I never tried before."

She nearly smiled, and then remembered the pages stacked on the sofa between them.

Wes grimaced. "Okay. No more jokes. Sorry. I'll go."

Part of Jamie, most likely the covert escaped-criminal part of her, wished he would go. But if he left, she doubted she'd see him again. "Stay for a minute. If you can. How long have you been sitting there?"

"Two hours. You stopped writing twice in that time. Once you asked me to make coffee, and I did. Your instant is awful, by the way."

"And the second time I stopped?"

"You looked up when I went to the bathroom. You don't remember anything?"

Miserably, Jamie shook her head.

Wes nodded. "You didn't seem to be … home, if you know what I mean. Like when you were writing at the store. Except now I don't think you're a writer, exactly."

"Because of Zane's phone call?"

"Because I read a bit of what you're writing."

Jamie only noticed that she was still holding her pen when she dropped it, and it rolled under the sofa.

"I'd better mention that you nodded when I asked if I could read what you'd written. So I read what you set down on the sofa here." He patted the pages beside him. "When I began, I thought it was a story you were writing …"

"It isn't, or not exactly …"

"But?"

"The story's true, but …"

"… you're not doing the writing. I looked at your telephone index cards. Different handwriting entirely. Same with a grocery list I found in the trash under your sink. Sorry, I was a bit sleuth-y."

"Did you understand what was happening to me?"

"Not even a little."

Jamie nodded. "Me neither."

The uncomfortable silence was broken by an unwelcome noise: a knock at the door.

Wes asked, "Do you want me to answer that?"

Jamie said, "No."

The knock came again.

"Are you sure?" Wes said.

"Please don't," Jamie said. "It's a rule I have. I don't answer the door."

"Never? Can I ask why not?"

Because I'm careful. "Because I work nights."

"But I ordered a pizza." Wes inclined his head in the direction of the front door, out of sight on the far side of the kitchen. "It's a hundred-percent whole-wheat crust."

There was no way around it without appearing unreasonable, even paranoid. She nodded, and Wes left her to answer the door.

Jamie strained to hear the other party. A young woman laughed, the door shut, and Wes returned and set on the coffee table a pizza box, a stack of paper napkins, and two litres of cola.

He asked, "Do you ever work days?"

"No. Afternoons until six in the morning, sometimes. Like tomorrow." Jamie took a slice of pizza. It looked like double cheese topped with salami and mushrooms, familiar to her as one of the Churley family favourites. She bit into the pointed end; it tasted better without the Churley family around her.

Wes said, "I guess you didn't have a lot of cheese in Vietnam growing up. I have a friend from Hong Kong, and he says he can't stomach it. I didn't think of it until this moment, though, sorry."

"Don't be sorry," Jamie told him. "Vietnam was a French colony for a long time. We ate cheese, and I like it."

"Do you speak French?"

"Some." It was one reason the Churleys had adopted her, and with the recent advent of cheaper long-distance rates, they envisioned a global network for their illicit enterprises. Her fluency in French and Vietnamese added two strings to the family bow. She changed the subject. "This is good pizza."

"And don't forget, a hundred-percent whole-wheat crust. Where do you keep your drinking glasses? Over the sink?" He had one in each hand when there was another knock at the door.

"Is the delivery person back again? I did tip her."

Before she could ask him again please not to answer the door, Wes opened it.

He said in friendly tones, "You two again."

"Right," a woman said.

"Sure," a man agreed.

Jamie stood up and strained to hear.

"How's your voter registration system going?" Wes asked.

The talk grew quieter. An older woman, a younger man. So far, so bad. She had lived with the Churleys for ten years and ought to have known the sound of their voices, even at this distance, but the corridor muffled the sounds. However, if it was them, creeping closer would court disaster. She set down her pizza and edged to the window. The chances were slim that their blue van would be parked outside, yet there one was, right behind Wes's Le Mans.

Would they have driven the old van across the country in their search for her? No one knew better than she the Churleys' hatred of change, so it was possible. Of course, they might have flown out and rented a blue van. If it was the Churleys at all.

Out of her sight in the corridor, Wes said to the couple, "Wait here a second."

He returned and asked cheerfully whether she wanted to come and register herself to vote. Jamie shook her head and sat back down on the sofa.

Wes returned to the door. "Leave me the papers to fill out and, er, they'll mail them."

He came back empty-handed. "They didn't have any papers with them. Some registrars, eh? And them with their famous system."

"System?"

"I chatted with them outside your building. They're doing voter registration around the hospital neighbourhood. They said they'd come back at a better time."

Jamie stared at the pizza box, motionless, as if the sofa were TS Eliot's still point of the turning world. As if any movement would topple everything around her. As if she would tumble out of this room, away from Wes, returned in an instant to the little bedsit in the Churleys' home that she shared with her beloved, dying young Churley husband. The ugly papered walls would again enclose her, and outside them would stand the big house, packed with Churleys and their extended circle. Wives, husbands, cousins: fraudsters all, some of them happily so, and some, like Jamie, without any options beyond cooperation or escape. And escape was a very dicey choice indeed. As she was experiencing now.

She'd been unable to resist the ghost. Maybe she'd be just as powerless against the Churleys.

"Have some pop," Wes said. He held out a glass to her, but she was sure that in her present state of anxiety she'd spill it. He set it down on the coffee table and added, "I don't want to pry, but I'm here if you want to talk about stuff."

"Thanks." Jamie's appetite made a shy reappearance. She took another bite of the pizza, and another. "I'm not good with strangers, I guess."

"I'll bet that's why you work nights."

"It's one reason."

"More shadows for strangers to hide in at night, though," he said thoughtfully. "Sorry, that was an unhelpful thought. But those two persons at the door are more welcome than not, because you want to vote, right?"

"I'd like to, of course." There were a lot of things she'd like to do, but getting onto a publicly accessible voting list was not one of them. She'd not voted at the Churleys', or been on any voter's list, for the criminal Churleys were not big fans of public access to their records either. "I'll wait until they come back."

"Gotta vote," Wes said with his mouth full. "That's not negotiable."

Wes held out another slice of pizza to her. "I feel like we keep skirting around the issue of these papers full of somebody else's writing. This Casey fellow. Tell me if and when you are happy to talk about it. In the meantime, I would like to say that the Italians wouldn't put up with this one-hundred-percent whole-wheat crust."

Jamie nodded and ate more pizza. She was going to have to leave this city and move to a new one under a new name. But not tonight. Not even tomorrow night. She had a little time, surely, to eat pizza with Wes. Another night at the hospital to visit Maria, hear about her tests, and play cribbage. One more day until she left her life behind.

Wes said, "I read somewhere that they have better flour in Italy. Do you think a person could buy that flour here, say in an Italian delicatessen, or is it like the olive oil, of which they say the best is all mobbed up?"

Jamie frowned. Did everything circle back to criminal families?

Naturally, there were safer subjects for discussion. "I had a lot of fun with the dogs today. With you and the dogs, I mean."

"Same."

A pause followed, during which Jamie tried to invent questions about the collie pups, but she'd already discussed their age, parentage, names, and probable adoptive families at the Orzalina home. At last, she said, "Let me tell you about the ghost."

"Okay."

"And you can tell me how crazy I sound. I've thought a lot about it, and I decided that I'm not insane, but I'd appreciate your view on the matter."

"You're not crazy. I read those pages." Wes said. "In fact, I'm the crazy one for not ordering more pizza."

"The last piece is yours."

He took the last piece. "Pizza isn't really supposed to be flat like this. In Italian movies, they kind of fold it in on itself."

Jamie set her pizza crust on her serviette atop the coffee table and picked up a section of the stack of papers. "It's time for an *if/then* engineering logic. *If* I'm not crazy, *then* I'm haunted."

"I must tell you that, as an outside party who meets a lot of crazies, I feel confident that you aren't crazy. Ergo."

"Ergo?"

"If you're not insane, then you're haunted. Congratulations."

"Thanks. Still, is it better to be haunted than crazy?"

"Of course it is," Wes said. "Haunting is an outside force come to visit, like an unwelcome house guest with no good grasp of boundaries. Crazy is inside you. It travels with you like malaria, and it takes a lot of curing, if it can be cured."

Jamie nodded. "But I work in a hospital, so I'd rather have malaria."

"Really? Interesting. I live with my mother, and we get whacko guests all the time, so I'd rather deal with craziness."

"What a team we are, prepared for either alternative," Jamie joked.

"Indeed." Wes sounded serious.

"Okay," Jamie said. "I'm ready to tell you all about it, if you want to listen."

"Right. We're going to need more pizza."

Jamie put the pages of the story together while Wes made the call. He returned and sat down on the sofa, a little closer this time.

Much as Casey had told Jamie his story, Jamie related her haunting to Wes.

One slice of the second pizza remained, and Jamie set it on a plate in the fridge with the leftover cola, for her breakfast. They nested the empty pizza boxes together and they folded them as best they could. They took the boxes out to the garbage chute at the end of the corridor and shoved them inside, where they unfolded and got stuck a few feet down. Wes fetched a broom and pushed the boxes further down, where they jammed tighter still. The chute was too narrow for climbing, and the pizza boxes were too far down to reach. Belatedly, Jamie saw the handwritten notice that read *Do not place pizza cartons in the garbage chute.*

Wes said, "That seems like it might be a self-rectifying problem. Eventually the weight of household garbage from the building at large will force the pizza boxes downwards."

Jamie's engineer mother would have agreed. But Jamie wondered whether leaving problems for others to deal with was becoming the sorry story of her life — just ask her dying young husband. "The smell would build."

"Same outcome. Somebody will push it down."

"I think I'd better come clean to the apartment manager."

Wes nodded. "I'll go with you."

The apartment manager scowled but didn't scold. He fetched a rubber hammer and his window washing extension rod, removed the squeegee, and banged the pizza boxes down to the bottom of the chute.

Jamie shook his hand. "You've got enough to do without me interrupting your work. I'm a night orderly at the hospital, and I know how busy your days must be."

The manager screwed the squeegee back onto his extension rod. "Is that what you do? Some people came around here and asked me what you do, but I couldn't tell them because I didn't know. You never wrote it on your rental agreement."

"What people?" Jamie asked. "Who wanted to know where I work?"

"Voter registrars," the manager said. "Earlier this evening. An older woman and a man, with clipboards."

"What did you tell them?" Jamie asked.

"I told them to come back and talk to the tenant of the apartment."

Jamie hesitated. "Did you tell them anything about me?"

"Just that you're a single gal of voting age," the manager said, holding up a hand in a display of integrity. "Was that all right?"

"Sure." Whether it was or wasn't all right, it was done. She reassured herself that there were a lot of apartment buildings around and about, and many occupants wouldn't be home. Undoubtedly the woman and man would note each one on the clipboard and check back again, like real voting registrars. But when they did knock, she certainly wouldn't answer. Probably she would be out at work or with Wes. And if not out, then quietly in, like a deer in the woods. A fawn's dappled coat camouflaged it as part of the forest floor, and Jamie was herself well hidden among the many *single gals* renting one-bedroom apartments in the area.

"Will I stay?" Wes asked. "I can sleep on your sofa."

"That would be nice — and fair enough, since I slept on your family's sofa," she said. "But this feels different, don't you think?"

"I certainly hope so. I imagine you'd like to take things slowly, build on this friendship, see how our personalities mesh or even spark?"

"Going slow sounds about right." There was no time to take things slowly. She had hours if she were sensible, days if cautious, and a week if foolhardy. She gazed at Wes. Foolhardy was looking better than ever before.

"Slow it is. I'll head home." He frowned. "But what about the ghost? What if you're taken over again at the hospital?"

"And what if he takes me over when I'm in the middle of dealing with a patient needing urgent care?"

They stared at one another.

Wes said, "Maybe you'd better stay home."

"But I'm needed."

"Staff shortages. Sure. Listen, it seems like you get a little warning before you have to start writing, right?" Wes frowned down at the pages of Casey's writing on the coffee table and the sofa.

Jamie recalled the pulling, twitching sensation that started things off, and how she for a time had resisted the force that had soon turned irresistible. "Maybe a minute or two. Maybe less."

"So you have a little time. Enough to get to a nursing station phone and dial my number. What if you telephone me to come and take you home from the hospital if you start writing again? I can say you're ill, which is essentially true, and they'd have to get somebody to cover."

"Would you do that?"

"Happy to."

"I'd feel bad calling you away from the store, and worse leaving the patients."

"You only get to feel bad about it if you have some control over the writing. Do you?"

"No. It's like throwing up. With fainting on top."

"Then it's easy. And honest. You go home sick."

A spiral of tension uncoiled inside Jamie, only to tighten up again when she considered how difficult it was going to be to leave this man behind when she ran from the Churleys. "Okay, I'll call you."

"And I'll come. But on one condition."

"Name it."

"Don't tell my mother about the haunting. If I know her, she'll hold a séance and invite the whole town."

Jamie watched out of her window until Wes had driven off in his Le Mans. Her suitcase was packed with essentials for escape and tucked at the back of her bedroom cupboard. When she did decide to go, she could leave quickly; her apartment was a furnished one, and she would leave everything except the linens. It was her practice, when she departed a place, to throw those down the garbage chute. When the time came, she could not rush this step, because she couldn't help picturing the apartment manager's chagrin if he discovered the bundled sheets and towels, stuck like the pizza boxes halfway down the chute.

At the same time, however, it appeared that the Churleys were refining their own hunt-and-seize system. They must have worked out that she would choose to be somewhere in a crowded neighbourhood around a city hospital. They were apparently searching via some kind of grid map and would inevitably find her if she stayed within its perimeter.

The balance between Jamie and the Churleys remained unchanged. She had to stay a step ahead. She must be ready to run without fear or sentiment. There would be time. She had her cut-and-run technique down pat.

Nevertheless, despite her faith in the enduring framework of her escape plan, something had changed. She had in the last few days come to enjoy her life as she hadn't done since childhood, when, after a day's labour in the rice fields under the hard gaze of the young soldier in charge, she and her mother would curl up together, talking, making plans, and sleeping well despite the wet heat and continuing uncertainty of survival. Instead of a quick, hard-headed cut to the bus station, she wished to hold out a little longer in this city, in the job she valued, with the patients she loved. She felt driven to maintain her connection with the Gates family, especially Wes, who was showing her what sturdy friendship and excellent company were like. Jamie had never imagined that men like him existed outside of literature.

Because of Wes, and because she was as happy as she'd ever been while in danger, she would wait past warnings and skim the sharp-edged zone of *too late.* This despite the advent of an odd and probably false confidence that made her feel that she might be smart to bank on luck and the cover of a large population to keep herself hidden. Even the existence of Casey's ghost, with all its unavoidable danger, at least showed that nothing was impossible. Mags and Daino might fail to find her; or Mags might die of some age-related illness; or Daino might crash the van; or best of all, the whole Churley family might, at the perimeter of possibility, be arrested and banged up in jail.

Jamie's mother would have approved the binary nature of her situation. *This or that, daughter.* Go or stay. Jamie would stay a little longer.

Monday afternoon at four, Jamie went to work equipped with a pen and a spiral notebook with a panda bear on the cover, obtained from the hospital gift shop. She hooked the pen onto the metal binding and tucked both between two bottles of cleaning liquid in a storage cupboard situated between the general population and the coma patients.

Maria's test results showed improvement, as did the light in her eye. She gave all credit to four successive wins at solitaire. It was her plan to press on with the transformative power of the game, and she refused Jamie's offer to buy her a new pack of cards, so as not to mess with success. Maria was winning again when the night administrator approached and called Jamie aside.

"A letter for you arrived here at the hospital."

"Oh, I'm so sorry."

"Don't be. I just hope it's not a job offer, because we'd like you to stick around."

"Give her a raise if you want her to stick," Maria said. "Money is like crazy glue for employees."

"I love the job." Jamie inspected every word she spoke for honesty. "It would break my heart to leave."

"Well, that's easy then. Stay forever," the administrator said.

Jamie held out an unsteady hand to receive a white envelope addressed to *Ms Jamie, Night Orderly.* No last name, because her last name changed when she ran. Even *Jamie* was an alias, similar but not quite the same as her real name, concocted by her and her correspondent.

She tucked the letter in her pocket, rolled out the supper trolleys, and served meals to the patients. These long split shifts meant that, comatose patients aside, most of the population was awake to wonder what foods they would be given in the little covered dishes, how much of the meal might somehow be picked at, and how much would be despaired of. She moved from bed to bed and took their minds off hospital food as best she could, describing the flowers showing in gardens she passed on her walk to the hospital and relating the plots of her favourite novels and of old movies she'd seen on television.

Her shift split just before the evening visiting hours began. Noisy or quiet, gloomy or cheerful, general population visitors were a loyal lot, but privately Jamie awarded the highest kudos for fidelity and endurance to the coma patient visitors. Some of these read aloud in hushed voices, and others rearranged items on the bedside tables or examined charts for a change in status. At about eight o'clock, one elderly woman drifted from coma into death. Her grown children stopped Jamie in the corridor to thank her for caring for their mother.

Jamie bought herself a cup of coffee to go with the pizza slice left over from dinner with Wes the night before. She found an empty corner of the staff locker room and dragged over a chair. She set the cold pizza slice, wrapped in waxed paper, on her knee, and placed the hot coffee on the floor beside her. She dug the envelope out of her pocket, pulled out the letter, and narrowed her eyes to read better in the poorly lit room.

Dear Jamie,

Talk about not taking your husband's name! You didn't even keep your own name! And if the name Jamie isn't a keeper, you can choose another alias! I suggest Grizaleena, after my great-great aunt on the Churley side.

Okay, you can stop laughing. And, speaking of moving on, our Aunt Mags and Cousin Daino are packing up their travelling bags and stocking them with string cheese, so watch out and get ready. This is your third move, right? So you must be good at it. Another day, another hospital job. Like you always say, anything's better than life with the Churleys!

I know, I know, not me. Not the good Churley! Haha.

I'm in hospital myself at this point, so I can write to you without the family knowing. I have help from a nurse named Brad the Handsome, who I literally trust with my life——and with your escape name. I wish you could meet him. Brad phoned around hospitals for me when I was on the ventilator. He found you.

And here's why. I don't want to freak you out, but in the interest of open communication between husband and wife, even in a fake real marriage like ours, I should let you know that the extra years I gained from excellent medical care are apparently used up. If it weren't for Brad, I wouldn't much mind.

Life's not been the same without you these past couple of years. I often wished we had run off together. I had no more romantic designs on you than you did on me, but we would have had a blast together building Life After Churleys.

But then I wouldn't have met Brad.

Listen. In about two weeks, or maybe three, you might feel a vibration in the lifestream, haha. Light a candle or something. Your last connection to the Churleys is tapering (candle joke) off and away.

No goodbyes. You know the name of that song.

Whatever you do, don't come here. We don't want to waste my one act of heroism, do we?

Yr Kam

At the bottom of the fold, a second hand, as different from Kam's as Jamie's was from Casey's, had scribbled eleven words: *But if you do come here, better make it soon. B*

Jamie set Kam's letter on the bench beside her. At the end of the row of lockers, a pair of shadows, one tall and one short, froze her in place. With a solid wall to her right and six-foot lockers in between, there was nowhere to run, if the shadows did prove to be Mags and Daino Churley. She made herself stare a little to the left of the shadows, to allow her peripheral vision clarify the shapes, and eventually they resolved themselves into a couple of coats hung on hooks on the wall at the end of the rank of lockers.

She picked up the letter and read it again. *Whatever you do, don't come here.*

And Brad's addendum. *But if you do come here, better make it soon.*

Brad was right. She did want to see Kam: to say goodbye, and so much more, before he left. In fact, she wished to walk straight out, rent a car, and drive the three thousand miles to the hospital where he was. She knew which one. She was less wife than friend, but she should be at his side. Brad could hide her in a closet when the Churleys came to visit.

Decision made, Jamie folded Kam's letter in half and stood up. In the meagre light, a sentence caught her eye, and she read it again.

We don't want to waste my one act of heroism, do we?

Back then, Kam had named his heroic act the *Sound of Music* getaway. He saved up his allowances due him as a true-born Churley and stuffed the money in a sock for Jamie to take with her. Next, they decided on her new employment. Taking work as an orderly was an easy choice, for under Daino's supervision Jamie spent weeks at a time caring for Kam in hospital, and she liked the work. Once these basics were covered, the cleverest, most dangerous part of Kam's plan was enrolling her in night school for a diploma in marketing. The family allowed her studies because phone scams were the beating heart of the Churleys' criminal enterprises, and they anticipated greater productivity from her. They got the opposite, for when Jamie graduated, she walked across the proscenium, accepted her diploma, and Kam's cheer followed her off the back of the stage. There she serpentined among the other students and their bottles of Baby Duck champagne, exited out the alley door, and ran into the night.

The bus station out of town was a block away.

She paid cash and changed three times.

So long, farewell . . .

Kam's plan had a lot going for it. Her new life was suited to her nature and abilities, and it was easy to set up and knock down on very little notice. In fact, as an escape from criminal enterprise that didn't involve the law, it had everything going for it except a guarantee of permanent success.

Now, headed for her third escape, Jamie sat back down on the locker room bench and took a last look at the letter. *Whatever you do, don't come here.* She tore the paper into tiny pieces and put them into her pocket for later disposal into several trash bins.

What nonsense, Kam's claim that the successful implementation of Jamie's *Sound of Music* getaway was his only act of heroism. As Kam himself would say, what a laugh. He'd been her hero since she was twelve, when the Churleys adopted her into their family circle.

Kam had risked his protected place among them for her. What if she reciprocated with her own gallant deed? The idea of showing up unannounced at his bedside sounded both right and courageous. But, if the Churleys caught her, all Kam's sacrifice and planning would be wasted. He'd die knowing Jamie was even worse off than before, forever stuck as the Churley family's traitorous captive.

Still, if she didn't go, what kind of a wife was she?

Since his teen years, Wes had likened his job as a convenience store clerk to that of a superhero, because much of the work involved dusting and restocking the Batcave while he watched the shop door and waited to serve. Since Jamie Stewart had come into his life, he kept vigil on not only the shop entry but also the wall phone. Here on his chair between the cash register and the Tootsie Rolls, Wes sat poised and ready. Jamie was like the mayor of Gotham in distress, and he awaited her Bat-signal.

The bell over the shop door rang, and a customer ran in. His hair was wet, and he took off his horn-rims to wipe them dry with his tartan shirttail. He made a quick tour of the store aisles, frowned, and asked Wes if he carried blank cassette tapes.

Wes stood up. "Sure do."

"That's a relief. I think a small store is the best store, but you can't always count on the music section."

"Depends on who's ordering the stock."

Wes kept his movements slow and relaxed. He took a plastic-wrapped pack of four cassette tapes from the bottom shelf of the stationery aisle and held it out.

The guy read the label. "*Perfect sound, keep crystal glasses away from speaker.* As if! No sound is that good. Can't I buy one individually?"

The guy's glasses were the latest in nerd cool. Wes shook his head. Everything had its limits, except possibly love and heroism. "You making a mix tape for somebody?"

"It's come to that. But I'm not completely sure, so I thought one tape to start."

"You'll need another three anyway. I mean, if the option turns out, you've got anniversary mix tapes."

"And post-fight mix tapes. Thanks, buddy. Ring it up."

Wes did. "Good luck with the tape. Don't break any crystal glasses."

"The mix tape's a winner. But wish me luck with the man."

"I do," Wes said. The door closed and the phone rang. He leapt a carton of Kraft Dinner boxes and answered, hearing his own voice breathless in the little shop, but it wasn't Jamie. One of the Orzalina sisters wanted to know if their order of pig ears had come in. Wes checked, and it had not.

"We're down to our last bag," the Orzalina told him.

"Sorry. See you next ear," Wes told her. It never failed to make her laugh. Hard on the pigs, though.

Wes stood by the phone and watched the door. Maybe Jamie was fine. Or Casey might well have taken her over. What if—despite their preparations—she fell into what appeared to be an inexplicable trance in front of a doctor? Or worse, a patient? What if Casey grabbed her right in the middle of a corridor or on the stairs? She might fall, and Wes wouldn't be there to catch her.

She had told him to wait until she called, but what was he supposed to do with this feeling of urgency to act? Like a superhero with a sixth sense for trouble, he couldn't ignore it.

Still, Jamie had been adamant: wait.

Now a woman with a baby in her arms entered the store and rocked back and forth in the beauty aisle. She squinted at the small-print lies on pots of face cream. Like her, Wes was trying to make up his mind. He wanted to respect Jamie's wishes; but how much more attractive and useful to be a hero. He could drive like gangbusters to the hospital, seek her out in the corridors, and carry her to safety. Protect her from the ghost who gave her nothing and endangered her for his own ends.

Wes attempted to picture Jamie in his arms, quiet and secure, gazing up with gratitude. But the image felt phoney.

The woman paid for the face cream with a grimace. "Another beauty purchase, another lie internalized."

"You're lovely with or without it," Wes said absently. He too was internalizing lies.

Jamie had asked him not to come unless she called. If he ignored that advice, ran to her, and took her to safety, he would be just one more person overriding her wishes. Like Casey. If he made his decisions and ignored hers, he'd be just like the damn ghost.

She had asked him to wait for her call.

He must do exactly that.

A small child entered the Gateses' shop all on his own and asked for a pack of gum. He was so young that Wes was tempted to refuse the kid's money. He wanted to tuck the gum into his soft palm and send him off with his allowance intact. Reluctantly he rang up the transaction, and the kid glowed with the power of consumerism.

The kid ran out the door with his gum already in his mouth, most likely against his parents' wishes. Wes saw in the child the glory of self-determination. It must not be denied.

Wes would wait for Jamie's call. Forever, if necessary.

He took a snap-off knife and opened the carton of Kraft Dinner to restock the shelves. The familiar chore calmed him, and the urgency to act dissipated. Strange that when a guy made the right decision, the weight of truth was most welcome, like the weight of a dog in your lap, a baby on your shoulder, or a lovely woman in your arms.

When three days had passed without a visitation from Casey's ghost, Jamie met Wes in the hospital short-term parking lot during the split in her shift. Wes brought hamburgers in a paper sack, and they ate them sitting on the warm hood of his Le Mans. She took a breath, made a false start, and at last told Wes about her life before and with the Churleys: about her Vietnamese mother and the American soldier father she'd never met, her time working with her mother in the rice fields, and her mother's death on the rickety boat on the voyage to Hong

Kong. She explained how Mags Churley had come hunting for a child to adopt and add to the family's fraudulent workforce.

By this point in Jamie's story, Wes had finished his burger, and she'd talked so long that she'd only taken two bites of hers. She ate some more, not so much because she was hungry but because her break time was running out and if she didn't eat, she'd keep talking, telling him about her long days on the phone selling robbery to gullible marks, and her secret midnights with Kam on the roof, talking nonsense about escape and leading real lives, laughing at impossibilities. Laughing in the dark, in fact.

Wes asked, "How bad are the Churleys? Is their business phone fraud?"

"On a large scale." Jamie nodded. "Scamming people who can't afford to be scammed."

"A family business. Like my family's."

Wes was joking, but he'd got it right.

"It really is. Mags's father was in with Ponzi and then split off. He moved north."

"The treasury caught Ponzi, didn't they?"

"That's why the Churleys keep it in the family," Jamie explained. "Families are strong. New members come in as children—born into it like Kam, or adopted like me."

Wes frowned. "Sounds like a two-tier system. Like, adopted family members to the back of the line?"

"I was lucky. Kam helped me. And then our marriage protected me."

"Don't mind me asking," Wes said, "but if you didn't want to, why did you go along with the fraudsters?"

Jamie studied the remaining half of the hamburger in her hand. "At first they tell you you're selling something on the phone."

"Cold-calling, like?"

"Yes, and it's good training for self-confidence and assertiveness."

"Okay. Justifiable."

"Then you start overhearing the jokes about the stupid marks. Meanwhile the pressure to convert sales goes on. And then you're meeting quotas."

"And if you don't meet quotas?"

Jamie said, "Kam didn't let that happen. Not to me."

"He gave you his numbers to use for your own quotas?"

"I don't know exactly how he got away with it."

"Your Kam is a decent guy."

"The best. He'd give me his numbers, and he'd laugh and laugh. *What a joke on Aunt Mags,* he'd say. *Here's one in the eye for Daino.*" Joking, sustaining her, and all the while selling robbery. Jamie stuffed the last of her hamburger into her mouth and chewed hard.

"Who's Daino? The right-hand man? The enforcer?"

"Also my promised next husband," Jamie said.

Wes stared, and the last moments of her break ticked away. Jamie thanked him for the burger, slid down off the hood of the Le Mans, and ran to beat the clock back to work.

On Wednesday night, there was still no sign of Casey. Although Jamie protested, Wes insisted on trading his shifts at the store with his sisters so that his free hours coincided with hers. The two met for breakfast on Thursday in a small café down the street from the Gateses' shop. Wes gave her seventeen good reasons not to go see Kam. Jamie insisted he change the subject.

Wes did. He changed it to Casey and wondered what might have happened to end a twenty-year-old's life in 1937.

Jamie frowned. "There was no war to kill him. Not until 1939."

Wes reminded her that the Spanish Civil War raged in 1937. "Men and women from North America, and from other countries, fought with the republicans. Hemingway went as a journalist."

"There's no hint of going to war in Spain in Casey's writing."

"He might have forgotten."

Jamie frowned. "Like losing your memory after an accident? Maybe."

"But whether he forgot or not, statistically there must have been lots of people dying of whatever killed him."

"Nobody's death is unique, except in the way each of us is unique."

"I don't know, though. Houdini?"

"He probably wasn't the only one to die performing magic. Anyway, I read he died after the trick, of something internal."

"True."

She led him outside, looked around for somewhere to continue their discussion, and spotted a small park fitted with a circle of wooden benches. "So even if we figure out how he died, that still leaves the question of why he's come back. It's not even exactly fifty years since 1937. Why now?"

Wes followed her into the park. "Why not now?"

"That's not helpful. But nothing is, until Casey tells us more."

"So now you want him to write again?"

Jamie sat on a bench and turned her face up to the sun. Wes sat down beside her, and she almost heard him wonder whether he ought to hold her hand. When he made the correct decision, she decided to finish out the week before leaving town. Today was Thursday, and her last shift before a day off would be Saturday. Then she'd pick up and take off, and visit Kam on the way to her next city.

And what if Casey returned at last and took her over in mid-flight? Disturbing as the thought was, she was worried far less about Casey's possible return than about her own departure. Jamie squeezed Wes's hand and set herself to memorize his features at rest and when he smiled.

Jamie and Wes brought Kaiser rolls and cheese to the Orzalina sisters and spent an hour with the collie pups. Afterwards, Wes suggested they check out the city newspaper obituaries for 1937.

"Gloria knows the editor," Wes said.

"Gloria knows everybody," Jamie replied. "And Gloria dazzles us all."

"There is no one she hasn't met and charmed, that's for sure. Your own mom sounds at least as splendid."

"That makes two magnificent parents. Is your dad great too?"

"If by great you mean absent. Do you want to search for your father's armed service records, too?"

"Let's stick with tracking down Casey for now."

Now was good. Now was nearly all she had.

They didn't need Gloria after all, because the newspaper office manager was happy to let historically inquisitive persons rifle among the rolls of microfiche for issues from 1937. Jamie and Wes sat in adjoining cubicles and scanned the reader screens until their eyes felt close to blistering. But when the last celluloid rolls snapped out of the readers, they'd found no record of the death of a twenty-year-old named Casey.

Time was moving too quickly for Jamie, and by now most of the afternoon of her third to last day was over. Wes took her for a cup of coffee before her shift at hospital, to reset, as he put it, all four of their eyeballs.

Wes had bought so much coffee for her by now that she'd sickened of Coffeemate and took it black.

She said, "Finding Casey's obituary was a long shot. Still, I learned a few things about hard hearts in the depression. Could Casey have been one of those unemployed men that flooded the city in 1937?"

"You're thinking that back then he could have died nameless."

"Maybe. It's a horrible thought."

Wes shook his head. "Toss that idea. His family would have searched for him. His parents, his grandfather, and especially the brother."

"Ted. Yes." Casey loved his family.

"Furthermore, and I hate to say it after our eye-boggling afternoon among the microfiche, but there's no way to prove Casey is even in this city."

"Or Dylan."

"Casey's story could be happening a thousand miles away."

"Or last year, or anytime."

Wes drained his coffee. "Please don't go all interdimensional on me."

"Sure, because that would be weird, not like being possessed by a ghost."

"*Touché.*"

Jamie laughed. "But I feel like Casey's close by. Just next door."

"I hope not." Wes raised his hand for refills. "Next door is a shop for men's socks and underwear."

Jamie drank coffee and pictured the quotation Gloria had painted over the archway into the Gates living room. She appreciated the wordplay but couldn't entirely agree with Tennyson's observation. *All experience* was not only, as the poet wrote, *an arch wherethrough shines that untravelled land*; experience was also an adventurer's anathema, a teacher that stifled daring and instructed in the best ways to run, hide, and gather no moss.

It was in Jamie's favour that her life had started out in the company of the smartest and most intrepid person imaginable. Her mother had kept them alive under threat of death and had engineered their escape from their captors against all the odds. She had died leaving a daughter to whom she'd taught English and French, and her whispered dream for Jamie was that she should someday be a UN translator, like Audrey Hepburn in *Charade*. Jamie wondered whether her mother would have been disappointed in her for failing to live that dream. But maybe not. For without her mother's bold example, Jamie would never have dared to leave the Churleys. And without the balance of caution she'd learned early in the shadow of the soldiers' guns, she would have been caught and returned to captivity and crime months ago.

On Thursday night, Maria packed to go home. Jamie smuggled cake to her bedside and agreed that outpatient status was optimal, and that Maria's health-giving games of solitaire must continue indefinitely. Casey didn't come for Jamie, and neither did the Churleys. Wes would be waiting for her at the end of her shift. All told, Thursday was one of the best nights Jamie had ever passed at the hospital, and her smile for Zane at shift change stopped that magnificent orderly dead in her chunky black sneakers.

"You happy, gleaming woman. What are you hiding?" Zane demanded.

Jamie was going to miss Zane. "I'm just glad to be off shift and heading out into good weather."

"Don't kid a kidder. What's cheered you up? There's colour in your cheeks, and you're an inch taller than a week ago."

"I've been walking a lot," Jamie said. "Must be the sunshine."

"The sunshine of love, I'll bet."

"Not everything is about romance." Jamie laughed. "Although spring weather does make some people feel kind of starry-eyed."

"I didn't say romance. I said love." A passing orderly tossed a Granny Smith to Zane, who handed it on to Jamie. "Eat the apple, Jamie. That's my advice to you."

Jamie tucked the apple into her pocket. It would come in handy when she hit the road.

Saturday, she arrived for a late lunch at the Gateses' place. Luckily for her, passions ran high in the best Gates manner as the family argued the relative merits of iconic horror movies.

Gloria stated, "There has been no further evolution in horror films since 1953. I give you *Invaders from Mars*. It's been thirty-five years since I saw it, and I still check the back of policemen's necks for small alien-controlled x-marks."

Riz said, "I counter with *Invasion of the Body Snatchers*. Donald Sutherland's silent scream is of the highest quality."

Jamie fingered the shreds of Kam's letter in her pocket and gazed around the living room at the Gateses on their sofas — all except Tiffany, who was under the table, miming how Carrie's hand shot out of the ground and turned every viewer's hair white in an instant. Dove and Riz defended *Poltergeist 2*, but their argument was poorly researched because they'd only seen it twice.

"Once," Gloria argued.

"We saw it the second time with Dad."

Gloria huffed and left the room with a tray of dishes.

"Our father is in New Zealand this year," Riz told Jamie. "They've been split for three years now."

"We're all taking it very well," Tiffany added.

"At least we are all on speaking terms with him," Dove said.

"I am not." Gloria stormed back into the room with a Sara Lee cheesecake in each hand. She handed around enormous slices to everybody. "I burn your father's support cheques."

"Only in effigy," Wes said.

Jamie swallowed a mouthful of cake and gazed at the increasingly well-loved Gates family members debating, justifying, and excoriating one another on their horror movie favourites. She had her own ghost and wouldn't care if she never saw another horror movie, but she longed to stay in this room, in this city. To stop moving on. To create her own life without fences and fear, in the daylight hours, and to choose whom she did and didn't want in it. No Churleys. No ghosts. Instead, she would populate her ideal world with the Gates family, the Orzalina sisters and their collies, Zane, and everybody at the hospital.

Jamie's gaze met Wes's.

I'd choose you.

He smiled, and she wondered whether she'd spoken aloud.

Saturday evening, in the middle of a shift, Jamie kept her promise and dialled the number of the Gateses' store with her left hand. This was an awkward manoeuvre, but her right hand was wrapped tightly around a pen and unavailable for normal movement. "He's back," she told him. "I'm writing, or, at any rate, Casey is."

Wes said, "I'll be with you in ten minutes. What if you telephone Zane to tell her you're going home sick? She'll come, or she'll get somebody. I'll meet you in the emergency waiting room, unless you want to go home and be possessed by a ghost in comfort and privacy?"

"Thank you, but no. I want to stay here, where he's writing. What if I move and he stops?"

"I wouldn't mind if Casey stopped," Wes said.

"I would," Jamie said. "I want a last chance of finding out what this is all about."

"What do you mean by a 'last chance?'" Wes asked.

"Nothing," Jamie said. "I don't know what I mean." Her overnight bag was in the staff locker room with her coat and wallet.

"I'll meet you in the emergency waiting room. Invisibility in numbers, right?"

"It's Saturday night. I might have to sit on the floor."

"I'll sit with you, then."

"You don't have to."

"I want to." A pause, and he added, "Unless you don't want me to join you."

Jamie almost said, *for this I do.* She corrected herself. "I want you to. Thanks."

She set down the phone and asked the desk nurse to phone Zane to cover the shift. She made her way to Emergency, holding her notebook across her middle to keep her hand still. She held out as long as she could against the ghost while she found an inconspicuous spot against the wall to sit cross-legged on the floor. Here she felt nearly invisible, and she wouldn't take up patient seating.

Once settled, she watched her hand form Casey's words at the top of the first page of her spiral notebook. The writing seemed more uneven than before, as if the ghost were agitated or even unstable.

"Casey, would it help if I didn't fight you?" she murmured.

Casey wrote, *I'm outside Dylan's*—

"Casey, I know you need somebody to listen. And I certainly know how that feels."

—*I'm outside Dylan's window*—

"There's something I've been wondering about. Well, lots really, but here's a big one. You have Dylan. I don't know why you need me when you have Dylan."

Her hand, all of its own, hesitated and then pushed the pen so deeply into the paper that here and there it cut into the next page, as if the ghost were writing with a small sharp knife. *I'm outside Dylan's window, hanging*—

CHAPTER 10

I'm outside Dylan's window, hanging here in the night air, near the streetlight in front of his house. He's framed in the window like a painting on the wall. If he looks up from his computer game, he will see me bathed in moonlight.

I enter the room through his closed window, stand in the shadows, and watch him. The television pictures flicker on the machine atop the bureau, and laughter hoots out of it. Dylan's concentrating on his other screen, the computer game board. His face is expressionless, and his fingers skip over the computer's typewriter-style keys.

I may have a long wait before he perceives my nearly invisible presence.

I study him. If I had some life to spend, I wouldn't waste my time the way he does. It seems that, even when dead, a fellow can't escape the bitter truth of life — the rich in life get richer and the poor in death get poorer.

I move into the beam of light between the screen and his face. "Well, Dylan, what do you say?"

He pulls back from his computer and bangs his fist on the wall over the bed. "Dammit, Casey, will you do something about your timing? I was just about to get Grand Master Rating Gold."

I know he wants me to ask about his stupid *Grand Master Gold.* "You make my teeth ache." Ted used to say that to me. "When you last saw me, I was snatched out of your front yard by a monstrous hand, and you were running away."

"You told me to run."

"Well, it looks like the dead person is the good guy, keeping everybody safe and facing down danger alone."

"Somebody has to, and I guess I'm no hero. Anyway, you look fine to me." He leans back against the head of the bed, propping himself up with his pillows. He's all in black again, and I wonder how his grandfather is holding up. "So, what happened with the giant hand? Any beanstalks involved?"

"So funny, I forgot to laugh." I tell him about the door, and his dark eyes light with interest. He even switches off the television and computer.

He asks, "What do you think is on the other side of that door? Is it Heaven? Or Hell, like with more of those giant demon hands?"

I don't know why I don't want to tell him that the enormous hand was shaped like my own. It feels like I'd be open wide to Dylan's mockery, and I've got enough problems.

For example, does some dark part of me hope to see the other side of the Door? Do I want to get the capture over with and surrender to the pressure to obey? Is there some coward's core in me that is willing—for Pete's sake, look at the symbolism—to *hand* myself over to the thing on the other side of the door? And then what? More time in nothingness, another fifty years or more of blank non-existence, after which I find myself back here, with Dylan an old man?

Or if I step through the door, would I be handing myself to whatever is on the other side of that door for judgement? In her last few months, my Aunt Loah often spoke of facing judgement and toiled to repay small debts and tidy every corner of her rooms before she died.

I wonder what I could have done that was so bad.

A rectangle of moonlight beneath the attic window lies at my feet, and I pace inside its shape, fishing among the memories of my short and shallow life. All I find are a few pale sins. Like cursing to impress some fellows. And the time Ted and I stole pocket knives from the general store. My grandfather made us give them back.

And once I joined some pals giving a bad time to a foreign kid in brown corduroys. I swear I felt bad enough about it afterwards to rate a little mercy.

If that is the kind of thing that deserves the door, then I shouldn't have been able to see it for the crowd of poor, unimaginative, regret-filled sinners fighting to stay outside. I shake my head fiercely, but it doesn't feel any clearer.

Dylan reaches for the television knob, like a drunk for the bottle. When I speak, he pulls back.

"Dylan, when are you going to stop wasting time with that television and find out how I died?"

"I'm not wasting time. I'm honing my detective skills." Dylan lounges back on the bed. "I've made a study of the television show *Murder, She Wrote*. It's my grandpop's favourite. Jessica Fletcher would kill to talk to murder victims like I can talk to you. It's a late-night rerun. Do you want to watch?"

"I do not."

"*Matlock?*"

"No."

"Your loss. But let's investigate. What's the last thing you remember?"

I'd never put him in the same bracket as Sherlock Holmes, but this is the right question, and I receive a flash of memory. "Second year at university. I started in September of 1937."

"What do you remember about it?"

"I know I jumped into university like a hungry dog on a plate of ground round, because at last I got to take journalism."

"Anything else, asked the lynx-eyed detective?"

There was this: Sorry to let you and the insurance firm down, Dad, but I was born to be a newsman.

"Ted was in his sophomore year at senior high." I add, "Ask more questions."

"Okay. What happened on the last day you remember?"

Recalling the day I died should be a difficult question for me as a ghost, but I receive a clear memory. I picture Ted, his hair a mess. You'd think he'd never met a comb. I gave Ted a bad time, but when I left secondary school, I missed him.

"My brother was with me, after class. Most days, if he didn't have basketball practice, we'd meet on our way home. I'd tell him all the ways university was superior to high school." I looked forward to showing him the ropes when he joined me there.

"This is good, and since you were a reporter, your observational skills must have been above average. Maybe you witnessed something that didn't seem important at the time but got you killed that day."

I frown. "I was working on my beginning credits for a degree in Journalism. I was registered in second-year English and Composition. Next, I wanted to interview to be a reporter for the university gazette." Sending in my letter of application and sample articles was the turning point of my life.

Did my journalistic instincts make me a target? It was indeed possible that in setting out to become a journalist I saw something I shouldn't, some assassination or treason, and was killed for it. After all, a real newsman travelled to dangerous places and met dodgy persons to get the stories. But I was not a newsman when I died, only a student hopeful, with painfully few assignments from my student editor. My adult life had hardly begun in 1937, and in the same way that Dylan knows investigation only from his television shows, I've only witnessed crime in the movies. But I decide to ask Dylan to develop this theory more fully. Any bone is welcome to a hungry dog, my grandfather said.

At this inopportune moment, Dylan's father walks into the room. I step into shadow. With luck, he won't stay long.

He says, "Your grandmother just got a phone call from the hospital. We need to get over there right away."

"I told you that Grandpop was getting better. Now you see."

A frown I read as *no.* "Maybe."

"Of course he is. He's been in hospital for ages, and the whole point of that is now he's healing."

"Anything can happen." Dylan's father hurries out through the door.

Dylan says to me, "I'll be back. Don't move."

He exits, returns, and adds, "Sorry. Think about what we're discussing. When Grandpop comes back with us from hospital, we'll pick up the investigation where we left off. Want the TV turned on? No?"

He leaves me alone in the shadows. A minute or so later I hear a car motor start up, and I move to the window. Below me the headlights go on and the car pulls out into the street.

I'm not waiting here.

I high-dive out of the attic window and move through the air above the car. It speeds up, and I sit cross-legged on its roof.

Once again, being a ghost seems to come down to this: a fast, pointless ride in the night.

I sit up here on the roof of Dylan's family car and think about the life I was meant to have. The life that was stolen from me. And let me tell you, I wanted to be remarkable. Epic, in fact, because I meant to be a writer.

I always meant to be a writer.

When I was ten and Ted was seven, I wanted to be an adventure author like Jack London. I decided I'd have a blue-eyed dog, half husky and half wolf, and we'd travel together to the Klondike, even though the miners' heyday was long past. But that didn't matter, because I didn't want gold. I wanted stories. So I'd talk to the old men about their youth in the gold rush, when truth was more magical than fiction, and the gold rush men hiked a rickety line between instant wealth and sudden death. Ted couldn't wait any more than I could, for he was determined to drive a dog sled through the blinding snow while I sat strapped in the back, penning magnificent tales.

However, when I was fifteen, hours in front of the radio news shows with my grandfather changed my thinking. The great North faded in importance, and I wanted Europe and Asia instead. I decided to be a newsman, an international correspondent for whatever newspapers would pay me to take risks and return with a story. That was living, and by twenty I knew I'd settle for nothing less.

My life plan went this way. When I turned twenty-one, and was taller than my father, I would wake early to leave a silent house with my duffel heavy on my back, because a typewriter and a thesaurus are a weight a young man can carry. My savings would be tucked into an envelope and pinned inside my shirt pocket for security. The ones and fives would look like a lot to me on the first day, but even so I'd be careful with my cash and eat meatloaf and cherry pie in turn at the diner stops, fully aware that a ticket from New York to Calais will take almost everything in the envelope. I would not be worried about being broke in Europe, though, because everybody knows cafés crème and croissants cost pennies.

And anyway, I'd soon be salaried, having talked my way into a junior position in a news service with bureaux in seventeen countries. There I would work to earn my by-line on wired reports, news I'd scoop first at evenings spent in rococo lounges and gothic lobbies of hotels not far from the arenas of international strife. Waiting for an editor's okay on the story, I'd lean against the open door of a telephone booth, eyeing the high-back chair that sheltered a prince or a black marketeer. In the evenings I would talk politics and poetry with accented women while somebody smashed glasses onto a stone hearth. In the morning I'd fly back across the water to take the first interview with a president-elect, and then dash for an airplane to Bombay or Mongolia.

By the time I was thirty, I'd be a prominent writer and adventurer. A man of the world. I would eat snake meat and toasted insects and never lose my poise. I'd feel just as much at home in a steaming Shanghai market as a Moscow side street at midnight in midwinter. I'd write cables like Hemingway, distinguish truth from lies, and tell that truth to the world.

For a year or two I might take time away from the news services and go to work for *National Geographic*. There I would vanish into the foothills of Tibet with a compass and a pack full of photographic plates. I'd disappear for months, despaired of by my friends and family, but reappear at last, thin, brown, and dressed in local costume, with a story from a civilization the world thought was gone forever.

I'd cover coups, coronations, and sensational trials. I'd fly with Saint-Exupéry and crash in the Arabian desert, playing endless hands of poker for matchsticks until rescued. In wartime I'd crouch in foxholes, with bullets snapping overhead, and scribble the soldiers' stories and dreams of battles' end.

Nothing would stop me from becoming a writer. No student editor's criticism, no professor's failing mark. I worked to succeed. And even here and now, half a century later, I remember my plans as clearly as if death hadn't stopped me short. Almost as if I'd really lived them.

But I never did, and all these years later, I yearn for the same success. In fact, and to be precise, I want my writer's life even though I'm dead. I speed along in the darkness and swear it again to myself: I will never give up. Because, if there's one thing a writer knows, it's that desire is stronger than death. And if anybody wants proof of that, they should look at me now, weightless and transparent, riding cross-legged on the top of Dylan's family car.

We travel along dark streets, and I watch the sidewalks and houses as we pass. Few people walk the streets at night in Dylan's town, so there's nobody to see me visible in moonlight, except one child at his window, up too late. His mouth is open in a silent yell. His fingers spider across the glass as he stares at me riding by as if on a magic carpet. His mother will never believe him. I wonder whether this young fellow will get the life that's coming to him.

Dylan's family car jolts to a stop at last, and I see we're at the hospital. It's a big white rectangle like a sugar-iced, store-bought cake. The grandmother and father climb out, the grandmother dragging Dylan with them, and they hurry up the steps to the hospital entrance. I slip down off the car roof and follow them.

Once I'm through the glass doors and into the hospital foyer, I look down and see nothing where my body should be. I'm accustomed to Dylan's bedroom, and to being able to see myself in his dusty, ill-lit place. But here in this bright corridor, out of the moonlight, I am completely invisible. The brightness makes me dizzy. As well, it presents me with a puzzle, for the light here is the same kind of hard, clean white light that shone on me outside the door. So, why am I visible there, but not here?

I must get my bearings.

I have feet. They must be about right there.

I have hands. In my mind I hold them here, well above the floor. And now that I've retrieved my personal context, I travel along the corridor after Dylan, his father, and his grandmother.

I remember the day my family took Ted to hospital with a banged-up shin where a lacrosse ball caught him. Hospitals haven't changed much since 1937. The lights are fiercer, and the walls are painted with rainbow stripes, but the smells of chemicals and chrysanthemums are much the same. The nurses don't wear folded white hats anymore, but we pass one wearing a cardigan sweater that hangs around her shoulders with the same old droop and swing as that of the nurse that bandaged Ted's leg and shooed us all on our way.

I catch up with Dylan and his family at the open door to his grandfather's room. None of them see me. I find a certain satisfaction in the thought that Dylan believes I'm waiting for him in his bedroom alongside his television and video game console.

The family enters a small, white-painted room, and I follow. Here is a single bed, tangled with cords and bristling with machinery. A screen showing jagged lines and circles hangs over the bed where Dylan's grandfather lies. The grandmother pulls a metal chair up to the bed and takes her husband's limp hand in hers.

"Kit," she calls softly. "Kitchener?"

Dylan's father pats his mother's shoulder. Dylan hangs back near the door. I see he doesn't know the right thing to do, or, if he does, he's reluctant for his own reasons to do it.

I whisper in his ear, "I thought of a good way to find out how I died."

Dylan blinks. He mutters, "Dammit, Casey, go home."

"Just go down to the town hall and ask to see death certificates from 1937."

Dylan scowls and moves closer to his grandfather, across the bed from his father and grandmother. And after all, my timing is not the best. I let him be for now and watch for my chance to get him alone.

Dylan's grandmother looks up and gives him a blank smile. "They say that sometimes they come back to themselves before the end."

Or after the end. I grimace.

Dylan says, "If you say it's the end one more time, I'm going to go wait in the car."

I look down at the old man. I should feel sorry for him, but all I feel is envy. He had his life. He spent his long years, fair and square.

I was robbed of mine.

I turn to Dylan, who is touching the back of his grandfather's hand. Before I can speak again, the door opens and a handsome woman nods at the visitors. She smiles in a manner appropriate for the bedside. "May I talk with you for a moment?" She glances at Dylan. "In the corridor. Perhaps the young man will keep his grandfather company here."

The older folks leave us with Dylan's grandfather. I gaze down at him and mouth his name. *Kitchener.* A name gilded with British military glory. It would have impressed readers on a by-line. Certainly, *Kitchener* would read better than *Casey* for a newsman, if he'd pursued that profession.

Dylan wipes his eyes with the back of his hands. His action reminds me that this Kitchener has a grandson who loves him. Who's determined to bring him home and looks forward to a future spent in his grandfather's company. I try to hate old Kitchener for his good luck, but he's so ill that it's impossible to sustain any kind of grudge against him. And perhaps I'm inspired by his long life, or his family that is so like mine, because a brainwave hits me. I know what my next step is. I ought to wait for a better time to tell Dylan, a less family-group moment, but I can't. This is too important. "I'm sorry to interrupt, but—"

Dylan starts and swears. Once again, he forgot I'm here. I hate being invisible.

"Casey, go away."

"I can't." I won't.

He scowls and crosses his arms. I do too. I have just as much right to a bad temper as he does. More, for obvious reasons. But the room is so quiet that it's difficult to stay angry. I remember that Dylan has never been dead, and so I pull patience around me and remind myself he too is going through hard times.

I say, "I'm sorry your grandfather is ill. But at least he's alive."

"Of course he is."

"Do they think he'll wake up and be fine?"

"He will wake up. He will be better than fine. I keep saying so, and nobody believes me."

"*I* believe you." I add, "Your grandfather will live. Tell me again: you're sure of it?"

"*Yes.*"

"Then I'm sure too."

He nods.

"So listen. Don't worry about looking up records in the town hall."

"Thanks so much, king of the flip-flop." His tone is not as bitter as his words.

Neither is mine. "I'd rather flip-flop than be a stubborn goat."

He half smiles. "Nothing worse than two goats in one small room."

"And, since your grandfather's going to be okay, please hear me out. I've just figured out why I'm here. I know why I'm back."

Dylan takes a breath. "You're exhausting, you know that?"

"Well, you're young and you can handle it. Listen, I think it's obvious how I was swindled out of my life. Your grandfather, lying here in the last section of a properly long life, brings it home to me. I should have had a long life too, and I was cheated out of my time."

"There's no cheating. You had very bad luck."

"Worse than bad, wouldn't you say?"

"Maybe, but you've got to admit that fairness has zero to do with what happened to you. Lots of people die young."

"But I've got important things to do, a career to pursue, adventures to live."

"So does everybody who dies young."

He's missed the point entirely. I wish I could shake him.

"Most people don't come back after they die. But I have. I'm back after fifty years and I'm sure it's to get the life that's coming to me. There's been a mistake made, and I've got a chance to fix it."

"It's far too late to change anything. And way too completely impossible."

"Wrong again. You don't have dreams as extraordinary as mine unless there's a chance they'll come true."

Dylan screws up his face. "Aren't everybody's dreams special?"

No. *Yes.* I look around the hospital walls, shiny and cold in the hard white light. "Be fair. I believe you about your grandfather getting better and coming home," I say. "Can't you see my side of things?"

Dylan turns towards me at last, even though I'm still invisible. He guesses right, and we stand face to face. He says, "Okay. I'll try to understand what you mean. Explain to me exactly what you plan to do."

I have only a general idea of what to do. I'm stuck for words, and me a writer. I scowl at the door to his grandfather's room.

It's metal.

The door. The light. My head spins. The fabric of this reality rips apart. I tear with it and cry out. Does Dylan hear me? I feel his leap, and I catch him, the way I did when we were flying. He folds himself inside my outline.

I hear him shout as we roll and flail through what seems this time to be miles of black, rocky gorge, sloping downwards at a terrible angle. But it's no relief to stop falling.

Here at the door, I'm real. I'm solid. Dylan lies at my side, his black clothes contrasting painfully with the light. There's nothing underfoot, and nothing up above us. Or behind. Or to either side. There is only the door.

"What is this place?" Dylan asks me.

"It's the door," I tell him. "Obviously."

I manage to sit up.

He stands up, black against white light, and touches the door with the flat of his hand. I shudder, because I know the terror of touching that surface. I remember the vibrations he must be feeling.

Astoundingly, he leans closer and puts one ear to the door.

"Music."

"Music? It's a trick. Don't be stupid. Put your shoulder against the door and hold steady."

I struggle to my feet. I see the door move against him. "Look out!"

Dylan steps back. What will happen to a living person if the door opens? Even if it takes me and he isn't touched, how will he get back to the living world without me?

And, if I'm taken, any chance of getting back my life will be stone-cold dead. I throw myself against the door and hold it shut. Dylan leans against it too, and I believe that he's listened to reason. But he's nodding to himself. "Voices!" and then, "Mom?"

"What are you talking about? Whose mom?"

"Mine. She's dead, too." He says it in a matter-of-fact tone, the way my Aunt Margaret would introduce a stranger: *I know you'll like each other, you have so much in common.*

He turns to me, holding the doorknob.

I put my hand on his. "Idiot! They'll say anything. Don't believe their lies."

He pulls harder.

The door begins to open.

I squeeze my eyes closed against the light and shove the door as hard as I can.

Dylan says, "The light —"

"Close the door!" I shout.

"I want to see." He pulls harder against me. It's not fair. He's got the strength that goes with being both young and alive.

I open my eyes, and we are nose to nose at the door. I'm pushing, he's pulling. The door is far enough open that he's managed to wrap one arm around it to the other side.

He says, "Casey, can't you see?"

"I don't want to see."

"But this light!"

"It'll take you, Dylan—"

"It won't."

"It will. And then you'll be dead, like me."

He gets the door halfway open, and the light cracks through like a hammer blow.

Dylan freezes. His grip fails.

Darkness takes us both.

§

In Issue 45, Winter 2025, read the gripping conclusion of Take My Hand: A Ghost Story.

LIAR'S LEAP

Jonathan Sean Lyster

Jonathan Sean Lyster *explores possible futures and alternative nows. His science fiction books include the stand-alone thriller* Oblivion's Wake *and the Martian Way series, with* Beneath the Sands Of Isidis *and* The Road To Elysium *coming out in September. Two more titles in this series,* Voice of Happenstance *and* Zephyria Launches, *will be published later in* 2024. *Jonathan's Armageddon Boys fantasy series includes* Judgment Daze, *available now, and* The Frog of War, *coming in early* 2025. *'Liar's Leap' was shortlisted for the* 2023 *Raven Short Story Contest*

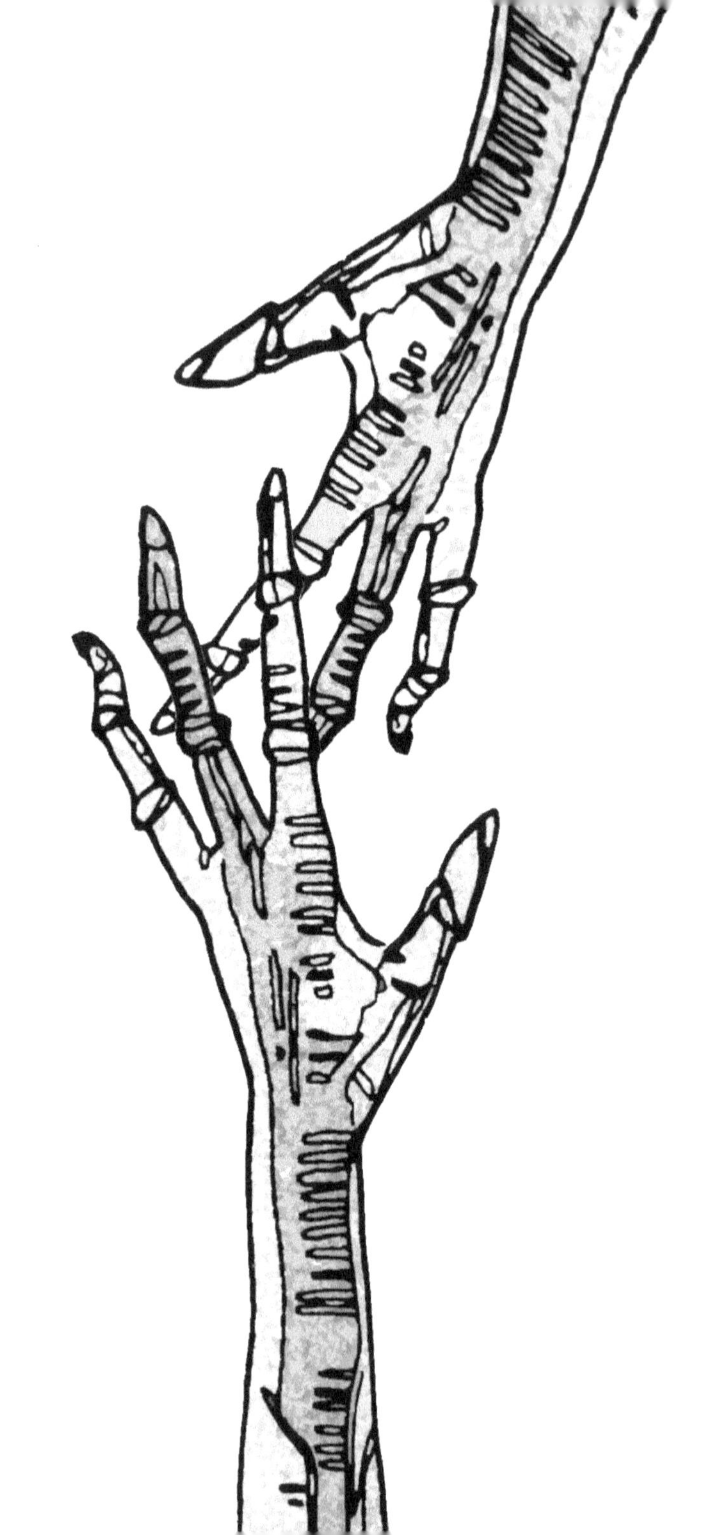

$\mathcal{L}$IAR'S LEAP

The sky is orange today. I say it to myself again, lifting an eye to the crystalline blue overhead. The second time I said it, the pain reduced to a short hot stabbing in my hind-brain. This third not-truth merely makes me wince.

My morning walk to the bus stop ascends a gentle rise. The view over the cradles where fusion rockets used to launch makes a saddening start to each day. The rusty hulks were abandoned when the Hiding began. One, just a jagged heap now, collapsed in last month's winds.

Even in my youth in the ocean, before my hand-feet developed, I was taught that fusion flares could alert the monsters to our presence. The interstellar gulf between us is no protection. We save ourselves as tiny brisprat do, by being hard to see.

One eye on the path, I position a second eye to watch for the bus. When the nearly empty machine eases in, I climb the ramp and settle onto a stool near the midpoint. I reach with my hand-feet to grasp the bars along the floor. Digits grip cool metal, bracing me for the ride.

The wreckage that was once a fusion rocket cradle bothers me. As the bus lurches into motion, I think about launches I have seen. We rely once again upon the ancient technology of chemical-fuelled ships. They lift from near the equator, use the spin of Home to help them reach orbit. The remaining gantries of the fusion ship port are lost to my sight as the bus gathers speed. Only the very old know what it was like to board such vessels, to leave Home behind and land in a twenday on another planet in our solar system.

We have given up so much to survive the monsters. Those around me accept that it will always be this way. Yet I cannot.

My suspicions have grown as my digits have lengthened. I look at my left-forward hand-foot. *Pretend,* I tell myself, *five digits there, not four.* The discomfort in my brain is mild now. Familiar, even. Manageable. I repeat the exercise twice more.

My bus reaches the university's entry slope. I descend the bus ramp and head to the Xenosciences building. Still deep in thought, I ride the elevator up to the Linguistics floor.

Zelep, my apprentice, is already on her stool when I enter the lab. She is young, with vestigial gills still present beneath her eyes. Mine were subsumed by my body before she was even hatched. Her skin is the deep green of the southern race, contrasting with my paler blue.

A single eye tracks me. "Jenap. Pleasant waking." Beneath the fading stripes of gills, her air vanes flutter with cheer.

"Good feeding, Zelep. Did you enjoy your time off?"

"Grecko launched a new symphony." Her limbs shimmy in remembered pleasure. "But questions have arrived for you. These are from the Physics department."

I give her a bow to proceed.

Zelep extends a graceful third digit to tap a button. The wall of screens lights up. I suppress a tremble, as I often must at first sight of the monsters. Their bodies are disturbing. They have four limbs as we do, but theirs are widely separated. The larger limbs appear to be used almost exclusively for motion, with digits tiny and deformed. Smaller limbs hang from a single pair of shoulders near the top of their bodies. These limbs end in digits like ours, though they have an extra. We have seen that this arrangement permits them to use tools while in motion, just as we can. They sport only two eyes, not four, suitable for parallax vision but little else, which explains why their brain-case is mobile above the body.

"Hyperspace," Zelep says. "The physicists are impatient for details. They say what we have given them makes no sense. The descriptions are inconsistent."

I slide onto my desk stool and tap into my console. The neural colony leader confirms that I have already sent every translation that mentions hyperspace. "What about warp drive? Have they made progress there?"

Zelep's digits flicker a negative. "The physicists claim none of the monsters' interstellar transportation methods work. And the gateways between worlds, the wormholes? The power to open such portals is more than the universe affords, according to all physics calculations. Nothing behaves the way the monsters' videos show it does." Her limbs jerk in frustration. "Their technology is so patchy. In some broadcasts, they use vehicles that burn hydrocarbons for fuel. In others, they harness anti-matter to power star-faring ships that exceed the speed of light. The physicists say this last technique is an impossibility, yet clearly the monsters succeed at it."

I fan my breather vanes, unsure how to voice my suspicions. If anyone is ready for them, it is Zelep.

The video footage streaming out from the monsters' world for four generations conflicts with itself. The broadcasts give records of daily family life that vary immensely. One shows a city not so different from how ours are arranged now. Another reveals the monsters' ancient history, the galactic empire they once dominated, apparently far, far away. They have weapons that can crack a planet in half or raze its surface until it is no longer habitable. They have settled worlds orbiting stars beyond their own. And yet we detect no radio signals from any sun but theirs. My work is to provide pieces for solving this puzzle.

It is almost a Home-loop since I acted on my suspicions and began to practise the monsters' skill. My theory joins together all the fragmentary pieces of information we have gathered. It implies concepts that are difficult to grasp. I struggle with it each day. We have no words for this. I have been forced to craft new phrases to express my hypotheses.

These broadcasts from the monsters are not-truth.

Centuries ago, Arghas worked out the process of evolution through selection. The monsters violate Arghas's theory. Fabricating visions of reality that are false, being unable to accurately see what is real or wasting mental and physical resources on concepts that are not-truth leaves a creature vulnerable to predators and competitors who do see the world around them clearly. It should make the monsters evolutionary failures.

Could Arghas have missed something essential? If these creatures persist in making stories that are illusions and have thrived, pretence must serve them in some way. Perhaps false visions let them see possibilities that are not true but can be made true. Of course, they might often find themselves making up stories that simply cannot be true, wasting mental resources. To offset this, there must be advantages to visualizing a world that is not true but could be.

Some broadcasts tell us the monsters went from rudimentary flight within their planet's atmosphere to creating chemical rockets that could reach their planet's single moon within seventy loops around their home star. For us, reaching our nearest moon was a 750-loop process. Sending probes to Lopa, inside Home's orbit, and then Fennha just a few hundred million xees farther from the sun, took another 500 loops. The now-abandoned settlements? Two hundred loops more.

My thoughts make my brainlobes ache.

"Jenap? You are mottling."

"I'm fine." I consider my next words with care. "I must share an idea."

She settles her limbs to her sides, focusing two eyes on me. "Yes?"

"It is difficult to articulate. Painful to grasp. It requires a different way of seeing reality."

"I am intrigued. Share your thoughts."

I point at the wall to the left of the screens. "What colour do you see?"

"Why do you ask? You can see the wall as well as I can."

"Indulge me."

"The wall appears grey in dawn's light. But now, in morning sun, it is blue."

I fan out my vanes. "No, Zelep. The wall is … white."

Her body grows rigid. A cascade of muscle spasms spreads through her flesh. I wince, knowing her pain.

"Jenap. The wall is blue at noon and grey at dawn and dusk."

I vent used air to ease the tension building between us. It works. Her flesh smoothes. I go on. "The monsters practise fabrications, depictions of not-reality. I am calling it 'pretend'." I struggle to describe the concept to her, take my time explaining. Her colour darkens with excitement. I press on. "Let us agree, briefly, that the wall is white. White as a cloud."

Zelep blinks rapidly, but the spasms are less now. "I do not like this."

"It is important."

She relaxes. "Very well. Let us 'pretend'. I agree, the wall is … white." Again she trembles. Then a gentle wave moves through her body and down her limbs.

I have successfully shared a not-truth. It is a giant leap for one of our kind. A first small step toward coming out of Hiding.

A FAIR EXCHANGE

Tom Jolly

Tom Jolly *is a retired engineer who spends his time writing SF and fantasy. His work has appeared in* Analog SF, Daily Science Fiction, New Myths, *and a number of anthologies, and can be heard from wandering storytellers if you buy them an ale on a warm afternoon. We were delighted to publish his story 'Falling for You' in* Pulp Literature Issue 37. *Tom's books are available on* Amazon, *including his fantasy novel,* An Unusual Practice, *the story of a doctor who unexpectedly finds himself working for the supernatural community. To find more of his stories, visit sites.google.com/view/tomjolly/stories-and-articles.*

$\mathcal{A}$ Fair Exchange

Amy was outside her shack, splitting pine logs on an old oak stump that she'd left there just for that purpose, its roots still clutching deep into the ground. She stopped for a moment to wipe her forehead and drink from a glass of tepid water. A large shadow passed overhead and Amy looked up, hoping for a drifting cloud to cool the air, but whatever had been there was gone almost as soon as it had appeared. Probably an airplane, Amy thought, though there was no sound of engines.

It was less than a minute later that the raven appeared. It sat, staring down at her, on a high pine branch overlooking the clearing. It cawed, sort of a low-voiced, gargling croak, not as obnoxious as a crow but not exactly melodic either. Amy took off her baseball cap, pushed back her thick auburn hair, and studied it. Was it another damned omen? She'd had enough of omens. The tax bill was an omen, foretelling a homeless existence. Her company pension, gone since the coal mine went bankrupt, was another omen, predicting that she'd starve to death eventually. Amy felt omened out. Maybe this one was just a bird.

It reminded her of her Uncle Derek's pub when it was still in business just outside of town. He'd called it the Raven and

Dragon and hung up a fanciful sign with a picture of a fire-breathing raven, its wings spread wide as though to fan the flame. Amy remembered saying, "You should call it the Crow and Dragon. It's got a better rhythm to it." Uncle Derek wasn't swayed. "Dragons hate crows," he'd said, without expanding on the statement, as though it had its own deep truth. The name stayed the same for nearly twenty years, but locals just called it the Raven. The pub turned into a gift shop after her uncle passed away.

Uncle Derek never made much money on the pub. He tended to give away a lot of drinks to his friends, which helped explain the debt. He always told her, "Enjoy life while you have it, Amy. Life isn't about accumulating crap."

He lived like he preached and walked the walk. He left Amy the shack he used to live in, along with a mortgage.

And now Amy had a raven in her yard. It seemed like a little more than a coincidence that a raven would show up at Uncle Derek's old shack. Ravens were smart. Had they been friends?

On a whim, Amy went inside, took an unshelled peanut from a bag in the snack cabinet, and put it on top of the cutting stump. The peanuts were starting to get a little stale anyway, she thought, but she figured the raven wouldn't care.

She could see that it was watching her closely. A curious bird. Its head was cocked to the side as though it could see better with only one eye. Amy shrugged. She leaned her axe against the wall on the porch and went back inside so as not to scare the bird away. She got a beer and pulled a chair up to the window to watch the stump where the tempting peanut lay.

Amy often measured time in beers drunk, and she had to wait two beers before the raven finally descended into the yard six feet from the stump. Perhaps it expected a trap of some sort. It hopped over to the base of the stump and peered over the top edge. Then it jumped up, grabbed the peanut, and flew off like the devil was chasing it. Amy chuckled.

The next day, while trimming the hedges along the dirt road leading to her house, she caught sight of something shiny on top of the stump. It was a pop-top beer tab. Odd, because no one had manufactured pop-tops for decades. She picked it up and heard a gravelly croak in the branches above. The raven stared down expectantly. A bartering bird. Amy had heard that some crows and ravens could be taught to do this, but this fellow seemed to have picked up the habit on its own, or maybe her uncle had taught it the trick.

She put the pop-top tab in an empty canning jar, wondering what other oddities the raven might bring if she kept giving it peanuts. Maybe she could start a collection. She took out a fresh peanut and put it on the wood-chopping stump.

Over the next few days, in exchange for peanuts, the raven brought a brass nut, a piece of tinfoil from a gum wrapper, a penny, and a bottle cap from Gordon's Beer, a local company that had gone out of business more than fifteen years before. She smiled at that and tried to remember the taste of the porter they used to make.

She'd collected fifteen interesting bits of junk in her Kerr Mason jar before the raven brought her a gold nugget. It wasn't any bigger than a pinkie nail, but it was a damn nugget. She held it up in the sky so the sunlight glinted off it. The raven looked expectantly at her, so she went inside, got two peanuts, and put them on the stump.

Back inside the house, she picked up the late tax bill from the table and hefted the tiny gold nugget in her hand, as if weighing one against the other. She wondered where the raven lived. With another nugget of the same size, she could sell off the gold and pay that bill, and she'd be good for another year.

Amy grabbed a pair of binoculars and went outside again. The raven had already flown away with its treasure of two peanuts. She scanned the skies for any sign of it, but saw only a few finches and phoebes darting among the oaks. Back inside the shack she fetched her phone and started looking up folks who might buy raw gold. There were a few. Most had 1-8 o o numbers, and God knew where they actually were, but she sure wasn't going to mail a gold nugget to them. There was a jeweller in town, though. Amy recognized the name. The shop had been there a good while.

She wrote down the address. Maybe if she got another nugget out of the raven, she'd go in and cash them in. Then pay the damned tax bill. Nobody ever owns property, Amy thought, they just rent it from the government.

The next day, the raven brought a shard of green glass. Amy held it up to the sun in disappointment, thinking for a fraction of second that it might be an emerald or something as rare, but it really just looked like a bit of glass. She put a single peanut out for the raven and went back inside.

The raven landed on the stump, squawked indignantly a few times, and left with the peanut. Amy watched out the front window of the shack to get a good idea which direction the bird flew. Less than thirty minutes later, Amy heard the raven's croak. It stood on the edge of the stump, looking back at her, and croaked again. Amy could see something glinting at the centre of the stump.

Amy stepped outside onto the rickety porch. The bird hopped backward off the stump, flapping its wings a little. She walked slowly toward the stump while the raven hopped cautiously away toward the edge of the clearing. Then it stopped and tilted its head, as if waiting for Amy to do something. To make a decision.

She picked up another gold nugget and shook it a little at the raven. "Now we're in business, my friend," Amy said. The raven squawked. Amy returned to the shack and fetched two more peanuts, reminding herself to pick up a fresh bag when she was in town at the jeweller's.

Over the next few days, Amy continued to trade peanuts for nuggets. Whenever she put any peanuts out, she walked into the surrounding forest, or around a few adjacent properties, in the general direction she'd seen the raven fly. Since the raven had left and returned with a nugget in under a half hour, Amy had an estimated radius and an approximate location. She looked up the flight speed of ravens and found that they averaged close to fifty miles an hour, so a half-hour loop would cover twenty-five miles and going one way would be ten to fifteen miles — less if the raven took a minute to rummage around for a fresh nugget in its treasure trove.

Walking through the forest gave her time to clear her mind and collect her thoughts. Where would a raven get a stash of gold nuggets? Sure, they liked shiny things, but gold? The local area had gone through a short gold rush decades before, but the creeks were cleaned out pretty quickly. There were still a few weekend panners who came out after it rained, hoping the dry creek beds would yield something new, but they never found much. It was a mystery, but one she could live with. The raven had gold and would give it away for peanuts. That's all she had to know. Peanuts into gold. Her pet Midas.

Of course, knowing where the raven's stash was located would be a big bonus, too.

After a couple of days monitoring the skies, she spotted the raven overhead, about a half mile from her house, and followed it with her binoculars for another mile before it dipped below the tree-top horizon. She noted the terrain where the raven had passed close to her, and used a paper map to draw a straight-line trajectory from her shack to the noted over-flight location, assuming that the raven would not choose a roundabout path just to throw her off.

The following day, she hopped into her old Ford pickup, left some peanuts out early, and drove ten miles out to the predicted location. 'The Lost Treasure of Blackraven Hill', Amy called it. She had a picture in her head of a dragon guarding a massive pile of golden coins and her hobbity self sneaking in to steal it all.

She saw the raven on her third day of driving and followed its flight with her binoculars to a dark spot high on the hillside. The spot was located behind a stand of gnarled oaks a few hundred yards off the dirt road—a cave, perhaps, the opening large enough for someone to squeeze through.

She parked the pickup truck between two low scrub oaks, hidden from the road, and entered the forest. The undergrowth was thick and the ground was rough, but she picked her way toward the cave, circumventing the thickets of blackberries and poison oak. Branches and briars tripped her up, and twigs and small dry bones crunched underfoot. More than once she paused and looked at the scattered bones, thinking they were a bit much for a raven, or even a family of ravens. A chill crawled up and down her spine, but she continued cautiously forward. She paused halfway to the base of a small hill, peering through the forest shadows to the cave mouth. She hadn't brought a flashlight. And someone might notice her blazing a trail through the underbrush. The property probably had an owner. Several other excuses came to mind, encouraging her to turn around, and she considered them all.

She rubbed her chin thoughtfully. The raven was already bringing the gold directly to her, with no significant effort on her part. It was a slow process, but so what? She didn't need a lot of money. With gold worth more than one thousand dollars per ounce, she was making at least three hundred dollars per day, good wages by any account. Minus the cost of the peanuts, of course.

She took out her phone, recorded the location with a GPS app, returned to her truck, and drove home.

The next day, she drove down to Jenny's Jewellery and Fine Watches. Amy wondered if anyone still wore a watch. The shop wasn't big, but bright lights were strategically placed inside to make all the shiny items jump. The raven would love it, Amy thought. The woman behind the counter nodded to her.

Amy asked, "Are you Jenny?"

The woman smiled like a salesman and pointed at a name tag. "I'm Carla. Jenny's the owner. I just work here."

Carla was slightly shorter and a good bit older than Amy, with grey hair tied back tightly in a ponytail. Her hands looked as rough as Amy's, and Amy wondered briefly what she did outside of working in a jewellery store. "Hi, Carla. I was wondering if you guys buy gold?" she asked.

Carla's eyes lit up like she was about to make a fast buck. "In fact we do. What do you have?"

Amy pulled out a small cloth bag that she used to keep dice in and turned it over on the glass countertop. Five gold nuggets tumbled out. Carla gasped and stepped back. "Where did you get those?" she asked suddenly.

"Um." Amy studied her. "The ground?"

Carla looked at her, then down at the nuggets, then seemed to get a hold of herself. Was she going to call the police? Ask her if they were stolen?

She did neither of those things. She said, "Okay, then. Wow, I haven't seen gold nuggets in this area for a long time. Let me weigh them for you." She picked up the nuggets and carried them to a small scale. "Raw gold nuggets are generally rated as twenty-two carat purity. I can check today's spot price online after we weigh them. And the store gets a twenty-percent dis-count on the price."

That didn't seem bad. Amy watched Carla weigh the nuggets.

Carla said, "I used to have a small mine in the area, some twenty years ago, till the gold ran dry."

"You find much?"

She stopped and sighed, staring at the wall in front of her. "I had a partner. We had a nice little stash of gold, and then one night he disappeared, along with all the gold. After that ..." Carla shook her head and returned her attention to the scales.

"Cops ever arrest him?"

"Nope. Never found him."

Carla looked up the current market price of gold, reduced the value for the lower purity, subtracted the store's cut, then offered Amy a price. It was enough to cover her property tax and fines, with enough left for a month's food. Things were looking up. "That sounds good," she said. Carla paid her in cash, and she left the store with a thick pocket and a request to "bring us more if you find 'em."

After depositing most of the cash at her bank and picking up some groceries, including a fresh bag of peanuts, Amy returned to her shack. The tax bill, along with a few others shouting for attention, was still on the kitchen table where she'd left it. There were food and coffee-cup stains on most of the envelopes. They'd been there awhile.

She sat down and started to write cheques. Each one felt like a load off her soul, and she wondered how she'd managed to carry all that weight around.

The raven had come and gone already, though Amy figured she'd magically appear if she heard the peanut bag rustling, no matter how far away. As she opened the bag, the front door opened behind her. She spun around, spilling peanuts across the floor.

Carla stood there, looking down at the carpet of peanuts, then at Amy. She lifted a gun. "Let's make this easy. You tell me where your stash of gold nuggets is hidden, and I'll let you live." She smiled.

Amy stared at the gun. "Uh …"

Carla waved the gun a little. "I'm going to tie you up. So if I go looking, and I find out you lied to me, I'm going to come back and make you wish you'd told me the truth the first time around. Sit down."

Amy sat down on one of the two dining room chairs. Carla tossed her a roll of duct tape. "Tape your feet together," she commanded. She leaned against the arm of an old sofa while Amy worked. "Now tape your legs to the base of the chair."

Amy obeyed. Carla walked around behind the chair, smashing peanuts underfoot as she went. "Put your arms behind the chair," she continued. She taped Amy's wrists together and ran loops of tape around her torso and the back of the chair. She stood back, nodding at her handiwork.

Amy grimaced. What if Carla shot her anyway once she had all the gold? "How do you expect to get away with this?" Amy asked.

"Why would anyone believe what you have to say? Besides, once I have the gold, I can just skip town. I hate that job." She waved the gun at Amy. "So where's your stash?"

"There is no stash. I trade peanuts with a raven. The raven brings me gold nuggets."

Carla raised an eyebrow. "You know, if you make up crazy stuff, I'll shoot you just out of spite. Places where you won't bleed out right away, so you have another chance to tell the truth. It won't be fun for you, I can tell you." She glanced back toward the door. "Hey, didn't I see an axe on my way in?"

"I can prove it," Amy said.

Carla stared at the ceiling thoughtfully, and the room was quiet for a minute. "Well. That might explain a twenty-year-old mystery."

"What mystery?" Amy asked.

"My partner and I were panning for gold in the area, and we amassed quite a hoard. A few pounds of nuggets. We didn't want to keep them in our tent. Someone might come by and steal the lot while we were out panning. So we hid them in a rotten hole in the crook of a tree, in a bag. One day, it all disappeared. Gold makes a person suspicious, and Joel thought I stole it all, and I thought he'd stolen it. But neither of us thought that some stranger had come into our camp and discovered it. Joel tried to pull his gun on me, but I was a little faster. And now it sounds like it just might have been a god-damned crow that stole it all."

"Raven," Amy corrected. "So what happened to Joel?"

Carla waved a hand vaguely. "He's long gone." Pointing the gun at Amy's chest, she said, "I'm guessing you know where the raven's stash is by now. It's what I would have done, tracking it down. Why didn't you just grab the gold all at once? And shoot the bird?"

"Why bother? The bird was doing the work for me. And the gold stayed hidden."

"A lot of good that did you. You should have waited until the bird was tapped out and cashed it all in at once. That way, no one would've found out about it until it was too late."

"Well, thanks for that advice. But I had bills to pay."

"Uh-huh." Carla drifted around the room, examining things. She came across the jar of raven trinkets. Next to the jar were three more nuggets. Carla picked them up, held one up to a beam of sunlight, nodded, and dropped them into her pants pocket. "Rather trusting of you, just leaving these lying around. So tell me where this crow's stash is."

"It's a raven," Amy repeated. She jerked her chin toward the map on the table. "See the line I drew on the map? It's about ten miles to the east. Take Highway 99 to Route 7 north, and stop at the low bridge about a mile in. You can see the cave mouth to the east, right about the tree line."

"Okay, Amy. If you're lying, I'll be back, and very unhappy." She picked up the map and pocketed it.

"Hey."

"What?"

"I still have unpaid bills. You want to leave me a nugget? After all, I found your missing gold, right?"

Carla pursed her lips, scrunched up her forehead, pulled the nuggets from her pocket, glanced at them, then dropped them back into her pocket. "Nope."

"Worth a try," Amy said.

"Hardly." She checked Amy's duct-tape bonds and left the shack. Amy heard the raven gargle some noise at Carla. Carla told it to shut up. The sound of her footsteps crushing dry leaves faded into the distance. A few minutes later, Amy heard the faint sound of a car engine starting.

Amy struggled, but only managed to tip the chair over on its side. By that time, she realized that her cell phone was sitting on the counter, and she probably could have reached it if she'd thought of it before she fell over. For that matter, she could have given Carla the GPS coordinates, but it was probably better that she had to do a little searching on her own. It would buy Amy more time.

She strained at her bonds. Night fell. Her arms and neck ached. The cicadas chirred loudly at her. Sometime during the night, she heard footsteps outside, and she shouted for help, but the bounding *tish-tish-tish* of a deer running away through dry leaves told her that there was no help coming anytime soon.

She woke with a stiff neck from lying sideways, and her bladder ached. The raven usually came around this time. It would be disappointed this morning.

The sky darkened momentarily, and Amy heard a whooshing sound followed by the clatter of claws on wood. She heard a croak at the window and twisted her neck around to see. The raven was tilting its head back and forth, trying to peek through the dirty panes. "Hey!" Amy called out. "Hey, Lassie, go get help." She laughed morbidly and wrestled with the duct tape until her muscles ached and she was panting, but the struggle just seemed to curl the edges of the tape and tighten the bonds.

The raven tapped lightly at the window as though testing it, flew off, and returned with a rock in its beak. It used the rock to rap the glass harder, and the pane broke. The raven squawked and jumped back from the shattered glass. After a minute, it came forward and pecked at the loose shards until the smaller pieces were removed from the frame.

"What the hell are you doing, bird? All the peanuts locked in here, huh?"

The raven hopped through the open pane. It spied Amy lying on the floor, squawked once, and glided down to her. It got close to her face, staring at her, eye to eye.

"Oh, please don't peck my eyes out, bird. I'm sorry I said that thing about all the peanuts being in here."

The raven straightened and croaked. It dipped its head, hopped in a circle around the chair, and stopped near her hands. It started pecking away at the tape. Amy felt the sharp beak jabbing into her skin.

After a minute, the raven hopped back a foot and cawed at her. She took that as a message and strained to move her wrists, which separated easily. She pulled away the loops of tape from around her chest and legs. By the time she was finished, the raven was gone.

Amy grabbed her shotgun from her closet and loaded it. Then she paced in the cabin for an hour, trying to decide what to do. She'd been taped up for a whole day, so Carla was most likely out at the cave now, emptying out all the raven's gold, or hightailing it to another state. It wouldn't take long; how much gold could a raven accumulate—or steal from miners, as the case seemed to be? It was weird that she hadn't come back to silence Amy however. Maybe she didn't want a murder on her hands, though there was already some doubt about what happened to her mining partner. Maybe Amy would be number two on Carla's kill list.

She stepped outside with the intention of getting into her truck and visiting the cave. If there was anything left to find, she wanted to get it before Carla came back.

The raven croaked at her from the tree stump.

Amy stared at the stump. Something glistened there. More gold? Was there still some stash the raven had hidden away?

She walked over to it, and the raven hopped away cautiously. It wasn't gold. It was something wet. She leaned closer, trying to figure out what the mess was.

It was a human eye. It seemed to be singed, as though someone had held it over a fire for a while.

The raven croaked proudly.

Amy turned her head to stare at the raven. It danced from foot to foot expectantly while she gathered her thoughts. "You're going to have to wait a minute," she finally said. She fetched a garden trowel, dug a small hole in the soft, dark soil, then used the trowel to carry the eyeball from the stump to its tiny grave. Sighing, she stood up and brushed the dirt off the knees of her pants. Was Carla dead? Or wounded and half-blind, coming back for revenge? Or helpless in the cave, trapped by whatever things lived there? It was best to make sure, Amy thought.

She went inside her shack, came back out a moment later, and carefully placed three peanuts on the stump.

The raven croaked at her again, and she smiled.

There were a lot of very small graves in Amy's yard by the end of the month. Eventually, the raven ran out of gobbets, or else they decayed before it could deliver them, and it went back to delivering shiny baubles.

This fact still confused Amy; she thought that the raven, having collected all the twinkling, glittery items in its hoard, would want to keep them. You could hardly call it a hoard otherwise. She was happy to keep accumulating them, though. She had two jars full of shiny junk, and she had coerced the raven to start delivering gold nuggets again. By her accounting, she'd stashed more than thirty thousand dollars' worth of gold behind a loose board in the wall of the shack. She'd taken Carla's advice not to just leave it lying around for scoundrels like her to discover.

The mystery of why the raven would trade its treasure for food came two months after they'd first met. One day, the raven brought along a partner, and Amy felt that she could start thinking of the raven as 'him' instead of 'it'. The new raven was, at first, tentative about retrieving the proffered peanuts, but she came around quickly after watching her mate. Two days later, two more ravens, dark brown instead of black, likely their young, joined the feast, and Amy found that she needed to stock up on more peanuts. She didn't mind. One of the young ravens took to sitting on her shoulder on occasion when she was outside, whether she had any peanuts or not, though the adults squawked when it did.

The gift shop in town that had replaced the Raven and Dragon, was having a hard time making it, and Amy, with her newfound wealth, bought it back. She dug the shingle out of storage, repainted the highlights, and hung the sign from two chains above the walkway out front. It took a month to retrofit the place.

The ravens eventually stopped bringing her nuggets, no matter the number or size of the peanuts she put out. But there was no end to the amount of shiny trash with which they continued to fill her empty mason jars. She set the jars up on a shelf in her pub and shone bright lights on their contents, which twinkled like diamonds. When people asked about them, she had a story to tell. Well, part of a story.

THE PROJECTIONIST

Lisa Alo Seaman

Lisa Alo Seaman *lives in the foothills of the Smoky Mountains with her husband and spoiled golden retriever. A voracious reader who dreams of days filled with long country walks, reading, writing, good movies, and buttered popcorn, she is currently working on two novels, one of which will be her first. 'The Projectionist' was shortlisted for the 2023 Raven Short Story Contest.*

The Projectionist

It was nearly dark when Boris left his lodgings near the city centre and headed to the auditorium. The blast of frigid air that hit him in the face never failed to shock his system with its intensity, and he tightened the scarf around his neck, knowing the gesture was useless. The cold always found a way to seep into the smallest opening and spread to his bones. He was always cold and would be close to numb by the time he arrived.

The walk was a long and solitary one. The high-pitched squeal and rumble of the monorail were the only sounds in the night. The ghost train. Screeching through the city with its passengers, who could only be seen in shadow as dark, lifeless shapes. He'd never taken that train, preferring to have his feet firmly on the ground. The train afforded him no protection. One of them was on board. They were always watching.

So he made his nightly trek on foot, past the steel-and-glass buildings that emanated only darkness. The warm amber night-time glow from lights usually visible inside buildings was absent. Past the open park area with its cold steel benches and tables. No trees. No semblance of life. Past the observation booth — empty now.

As if summoned by his thoughts, one of them was just around the corner. His heart beat harder and faster with each step, the anticipation of the encounter fuelling his flight response. Tonight, just a nod from the man. An acknowledgement that he was there but would allow Boris to continue on his way.

As he passed the man, Boris dared to look up and meet his eyes. Not a friendly face, but not menacing either. So Boris reciprocated with his own nod. He was useful to them now. His nightly newsreel presentations and lectures provided them with information they wanted.

It was close. Just over the small hill, in the side entrance and up the stairs to the projection booth. For a couple of hours, a respite from the cold and loneliness. The historian in him loved to look through the canisters of film stored on metal shelves. His world was in that little room. He didn't mind the confinement of the booth. Like a dog in a crate, he felt safer in a tight, dark space.

The side door was open for him. Mareen would already be there setting up equipment. She greeted him with a warm smile and handed him a hot beverage. The liquid felt like molten lava sliding down his throat, warming his insides inch by inch. He smiled back, sensing that Mareen understood all that he meant to convey.

He climbed the stairs and entered the booth. He had methodically planned his lessons. Two hours was not enough to cover any one subject, but each night he was able to show something that, taken together with the rest, would depict a picture of humanity and the depths to which it could sink.

With a surgeon's precision, he slowly and reverently threaded the film through the projector. He could hear the crowd beginning to gather below. Soon Mareen's translations would appear alongside the screen. Each evening, he had to record his narration and lecture for the following evening's presentation. He pressed a button in his booth and the auditorium lights went out and the images began to appear on the screen.

Laughing young men throw books into bonfires — one after another, treasures by Hemingway, Freud, Einstein, Sinclair, and Keller.

Around the world, *The Satanic Verses* burn.

In Timbuktu, a library holding ancient manuscripts is destroyed.

He could feel the wetness on his cheeks, tears that he was unable to control. For the evil present in some men, the ignorance of others, and the futility of his situation. He still couldn't remember how he ended up here, or how long it had been.

Mareen's translations continued, and he knew she had reached his lecture about book burnings and book bannings that weren't always covered on film. Occasionally, one of the audience would look up at the booth. When Mareen was finished, Boris stepped out of the booth and watched as they very quietly filed out of the auditorium, most giving the slightest nod to him. He always acknowledged the recognition.

He returned to his booth and continued his work, contemplating the next lesson. He dictated the narration for the newsreel, and then his lecture, handing it to Mareen with a smile as he left.

If possible, it was colder than before, and the sky had a strange pink tint. He started his long walk back, shivering and tugging at his coat. Then, because he couldn't help himself, he looked up to that pink sky. The moon to the right was a shimmering gold, the left was pale yellow, and the third moon, directly above, was somewhere in between.

A WEAVER'S WEB

Barry Charman

Barry Charman is a writer living in North London. He has been published in various magazines and anthologies, including Ambit, Griffith Review, The Ghastling, and Popshot Quarterly. *His* poems have appeared most recently with The Literary Hatchet and The Linnet's Wings. Doom Warnings, *Barry's self-published collection of strange and speculative short stories, will soon be available on Amazon. Visit him at barrycharman.blogspot.co.uk.*

A Weaver's Web

Deep within Lovelock Woods, down in the wild weird lands, there stood a mansion so dark even moonlight from three moons could barely pick it out.

It sat like a hunched creature. Intermittent lights escaped its heavily draped windows, while cries of revelry escaped into the pitch-black night, as if they were fleeing for their lives. Roads that led to the mansion were treacherous. Straying from the paths was lethal. But the parties were worth it. Usually. Deadsy's gatherings were the stuff of legend, and he wouldn't throw a party anywhere else.

Home was for the heartless.

Dullard Sixpence was hiding under the bed when he heard the first shot.

"Bullets," he muttered sheepishly. "Bit allergic."

Next to him, the woman he'd startled scowled. She was a spider-tamer, got all of the crawlies in check for creeping out of line, probably part of Bawd's entourage.

He smiled awkwardly. "If you've not just come for the murder, I'd recommend the punch."

A spider was running over the back of her hand. She paused it with a look, and frowned. "What's in it?"

Sixpence pulled a face. "Indescribable. But the best things are."

She nodded at her spiders, who appeared to be listening attentively. "A truth. Worse has been woven from less."

He watched as the spiders waved their little legs.

"So . . ." He nodded at the door across from the bed, indicating the sounds that were peppering the mansion. "Sounds like a bit of a do."

She sighed. "Bawd Deadsy is a terrible host if you don't want to die."

He put out his hand. "Dullard Sixpence. I was the guy that brought all the ghosts."

Her eyes narrowed. "Oh, you're a collector?"

"A dabbler. They really liven things up . . . pardon the pun."

His hand was still extended. She paused, then shook it. "Willow Widow."

They shared a moment that deflated of its own accord. "Guess we're stuck here," he muttered, "till the dying dies down."

She puffed her cheeks out. "So gaudy."

"I know, right? Seventh son of a man who stabbed a seventh son, thinks he's got a loophole from the Devil himself. Gets up to all sorts. *All sorts.* It's not on, frankly."

Willow wriggled her fingers, and the spiders began weaving something. For her? She whispered, "Idle hands."

"I guess." He wondered if she meant Deadsy or herself.

They listened as heavy footsteps chased light feet past the door. Sixpence winced, then wondered whose room they were in. He didn't know the name of the person whose bed he was going to die under, and it seemed improper. Whose mansion was it, anyway? Had they been in on the climax, or lured to some lurid demise?

The guests had lurched into Bawd's party from all walks of life. Sixpence wondered what any of them had expected from the festivities. There'd been a ball, tricks, entertainments, all generally opulent. Had Bawd planned for it to pop this way, or had he just got bored?

Well, Sixpence's ghosts had given people a fun runaround, at least. He propped his head in his palm. "Normally, I just collect disturbed spirits. They're good talkers except the screamers. They get a bit lonely, so you're doing them a favour, really."

"Mmm." Willow was staring intently as the spiders continued weaving. She wriggled her fingers, and they seemed to follow her directions.

"What are they making?"

"Might be something useful. Where are your ghosts? Can't they muck in?"

He hesitated. "They'll be bouncing off the walls. They like a good spookshow. Most fun they get."

"Where do you keep them?"

Sixpence watched a shadow move under the door, and lowered his voice. "Well, they're just lights now, so you keep them in a dark moment."

Her voice dropped with his. "What's a dark moment?"

He tried to indicate a shape with his hands, but his elbows couldn't find room. "Obsidian flask, so big. Hard to come by, usually have to find them in Viking wreckage."

She looked suddenly animated. "Did you know *Viking* was a verb?"

"Uh, I did not."

"It was an activity. You *went* viking. Words weave into all kinds of meanings over time …"

There was enough light for him to make out her face, pale and surprisingly engaged. Her eyes were hazel, but the darkness gave them a greenish tint. He realized he was staring. "Are there any green spiders?"

Her smile had been faltering, but now it lit back up. "The common garden spider is green, and the green lynx spider, of course, and the orb-weaver——"

He grinned. "Neat."

Outside, they heard Bawd Deadsy scream at a reveller, "Stop in your tracks and get shot like a lady!"

Willow sighed. "And when he gets bored of murder, what then? Charity, I suppose."

"More money than marbles."

She nodded. "And a coffin-shaped heart. Everything's got to be as dead as him inside."

"Think we're safe here?"

"Under the bed?" She looked at the spiders and raised her eyebrows. "He asks if we're safe."

The spiders twitched.

"We could break the window, maybe," she suggested. "Can't be that high."

"High enough."

Sixpence rapped his fingers against the burgundy carpet. "I can't die here——I promised the ghosts a picnic. Without me, they won't even stick together; they'll probably just evaporate."

"They might prefer it."

He tried not to sound offended. "I'm good company. Usually."

"I mean, don't they have somewhere to be?"

"*That*, I don't ask. Flirting with indiscretion, frankly."

She was considering this when the door across from them suddenly creaked open. Bawd Deadsy stepped into the room, red footprints and all. All they could see were his soiled socks and tapping toes. He was old enough to be as callous as he was rich, but young enough to need telling.

"Right. Anyone in here gonna make me wait?"

Willow flexed her web, and Sixpence gaped. Before he could ask, *Is that a gun that shoots spiders?* she'd let off a round.

Bawd went down howling. Sixpence took the opportunity to reach out and deck him, then called for any nearby ghost to sit on him till he fell quiet. Maud Sullivan, passing poltergeist, hurried through the wall and duly obliged.

They got out from under the bed and studied each other. Sixpence watched the spiders run up Willow's white dress and line up on her shoulder. They seemed to be studying him, almost protectively. "You off, then?"

"This party isn't for me."

He nodded. "You know, there's a tavern down the road. Very cobwebby sort of joint."

Leaving Deadsy whimpering petulantly behind them, they walked out, followed by spiders and ghouls, some of whom Sixpence had brought, some of whom he hadn't.

The ghosts welcomed the dazed newcomers, while the spiders gestured to friends as they passed them. The unusual procession left the mansion and followed a snaking driveway down to two black gates.

Sixpence promised Willow ghosts that crawled, for there were wayward spirits everywhere, and there was no lack of lonely spiders, even in death. She would give them aid, companionship. He felt something weaving them closer together.

All in all, worse had been woven from less.

The road they took was courted by moonlight and bordered by tall trees that leaned forward as if listening. It cut through an ancient, dense woodland. There were no other buildings here, no trace of civilization, just the yawning world and the texture of its dreams.

Sixpence worried for his caravan, hidden across the woods in the undergrowth by an old creek. He'd left a wailing banshee on watch; probably all it had done was upset a few squirrels. He hoped nobody stumbled across it. All he had in the world was tucked away on its dusty shelves. A small home, it seemed smaller the more he thought about it.

The night was cool, ethereal in its calm. Thinking this, Sixpence felt a stinging sensation tiptoe around him. It felt unnatural. He twisted around. "Did — Did something brush past me?"

Willow glanced at him. "There's a hitcher in your shadow."

He stopped. "A what?"

"A shadow's climbed onto yours. Hitching. He'll probably jump off down the road."

"What if he doesn't?"

She grimaced.

Sixpence frowned, and they continued walking. "It's an old country, this." He sighed. "Older than most."

Willow skipped over a puddle. "True. The leaves are still rustling. Still speaking the oldest song. Most places, the trees aren't even standing any longer."

"You been here long?"

She turned a palm, watching two spiders that were dancing in her hand. "I follow the seasons when they turn."

He glanced over a shoulder. His indistinct phantoms were strolling behind them. Sometimes they'd stop and gesture, pointing something out for the rest. They seemed to find an endless fascination with the world. The moonlight washed through them like pale blades. At their feet, spiders walked in Willow's wake.

Sixpence wasn't sure what to say. "You're not like most girls I've met."

Willow pulled her white shawl closer around her shoulders and shrugged. "You've been hiding under the wrong beds."

He smiled. "I can see that."

Ageing and crooked trees lined the road. Willow was looking at them, tilting her head at twigs that were snapping.

Sixpence noticed. "Anything out there?"

She didn't look back, just nodded. "The night's busy."

Groaning, he wondered if there'd even be room at the tavern. He'd noticed it on his way up to the mansion, picked it out as a spot to find a cosy corner to wind down in. Of course, the party had turned out to offer more complications than coins. He felt around in his pocket. Did he even have enough to fill a flagon?

"It's not far," he said.

Deep footprints dotted the sodden ground ahead, each filled with a small volume of rainwater. The road became muddy, and Willow trod more carefully. A light rain began to come down. Willow turned to her spiders and made a few swift gestures with her hands. They left the road and returned with small leaves they used to cover themselves.

"How do you do that?" Sixpence asked. "How do you even *learn* to do that?"

"You learn to listen."

She made it sound easy. "Is that all?"

Willow glanced at him. "Hardest thing in the world to do properly, listen."

He thought about that. If listening were easy, people wouldn't have things to fight wars over. "Easy thing to overlook," he muttered, and caught her nodding from the corner of his eye.

He wondered, then, about the shadow that had hitched a ride. If it spoke, how would you hear it?

What would it say?

Slowing his breathing, he let his steps come naturally. He forgot about Willow's green eyes and the ghouls that muttered behind him. He ignored the rain as it came down and tried to tune his mind to hear anything that might speak between the drops.

"*. . . Deadsy . . .*"

His eyes had been closing, but now they shot open.

"*What?*" he thought.

"*Deadsy will follow. Drop me off at the crossroads. I'd like to be on my way.*"

Sixpence shivered. He wondered what it would do if he changed direction.

"*I'd peel you from the inside out.*"

The thoughts, not his own, whispered through his head and unnerved him. Sixpence quickened his step. God, he needed to get off this road.

"Come back!"

He turned, startled by the crisp note of panic suddenly in Willow's voice. Following her gaze, he saw some of the spiders had wandered off the path and diverted deep into the woods. The rain must have confused them. The darkness there was dense. An uninvited sensation joined him on the road. The night shivered, and the rain tasted brackish, tainted.

Dark shapes in the trees shuddered.

The separated spiders hesitated. Darkness crept around them until they were cut off. Sixpence grimaced. They looked done for. Willow took a step forward, and he reached out to her. "Careful. I don't like to think what Deadsy's drawn here."

"No, you wouldn't," the shadow chuckled.

Four spiders were trapped on a rock. They seemed stricken, and their little legs signalled to each other uncertainly. Willow didn't take her eyes from them. "I promised I'd take care of them …" she said.

Promises were often more fragile than one knew, but he didn't say this.

She crouched down and began signing to a group of spiders that had gathered around her. He wondered if she was going to ask them to make a lasso or something.

Willow shook her head. Apparently there was discord.

Time, he realized. The spiders were too far out. The woods were a treacherous place, whether you were living or dead. It wasn't safe to linger, and you should never get lost. There might be things out there only *he* could see. It had never occurred to him before to try and convene with a spider's ghost.

He signalled over to one of his ghouls and pointed out the spiders' situation. The darkness around them was *uncurling* in a way that was almost uncomfortable.

The ghoul—once a pastor, Sixpence believed—looked at the spiders and wrinkled a translucent nose.

"Any *other* spiders out there?"

The pastor got where he was coming from, shot him a bemused look, and waded into the darkness.

"Let *me* try," Sixpence said, as Willow watched.

His ghoul crouched down, searched, then found some pale ethereal creature crawling at its feet. He stooped, and some manner of explanation took place. Even so, the darkness came around them like a tide, drowning all.

"Deadsy came for the winters," Willow muttered.

Beside her, Sixpence nodded. "Can't imagine what died here to let so much *rot* feel comfortable ..."

The pastor reappeared, leading an odd trail of phantom spiders. They'd found the others and were leading them back. From the encroaching darkness, something reached out and put a claw-like hand on the ghoul's shoulder. He stopped immediately.

"Bad touch."

"Be careful!" Sixpence shouted.

The pastor shivered. It was unusual to see one of them react in so human a way. Abruptly, he turned and began walking back into the darkness.

"Wait!" Sixpence called.

"Too late."

The ghoul was soon no more than a pale light fluttering in a receding abyss. The pastor had been with him for so long, Sixpence didn't know what to say. He just stared, waiting. But nothing moved. Nothing stirred.

Willow was crouching by her spiders. They'd all made it back to her. She looked up. "I'm sorry, what happened?"

Sixpence couldn't answer, so he turned away from the dark and wondered if the dead always found their way home.

When they finally came to a crossroads, they ignored a scarecrow giggling in some stocks and turned left. The tavern appeared ahead of them — a pile of rustic beams jutting towards a smoking chimney. A fire within gave the window a warm glow. The closer they got, the louder the hum of conversation and laughter became.

The shadow had fallen silent. Sixpence hoped that meant it had jumped off. The itch had left him, at least.

He looked around for something to keep the ghouls entertained. There was an old tree across the road from the tavern, and ghosts were drawn to ancient things that hadn't died yet. He pointed at it, then watched as they wandered off, surrounding the tree with a sort of disrespectful reflection.

Willow's spiders ran up her cloak and disappeared. She looked at the building, tilting her head as she read the sign. "The Unravelled Traveller."

Sixpence grinned. "More a comment on the effect of the roads than anything else."

They paused inside the doorway. The inn was filled to the brim with night walkers and wayward fellows. Sixpence instinctively clutched his purse closer and gave the room a stealthy vibe check.

In answer, two tentacled highwaymen threw down in a corner, which was illuminated by the dance of their daggers. Two women brawled by the bar, and their tattoos writhed and exchanged the most vile insults. As they went down, another woman stepped over them and ordered a bowl of witch-tear soup. The bartender blinked at none of it.

Damn fine establishment all round. Sixpence shrugged. He nodded towards a table in an empty booth. "Get you a drink?"

Willow was admiring the texture of a tablecloth, brushing the material with long fingers. "Everything here is ruined, yet preserved at the point of deterioration."

Decay was often in fashion when it got a rustic enough hue. She wandered over to the booth and sat, while Sixpence arranged for some flagons and food to be brought over. When he was done, his purse felt almost empty.

His ghouls were meant to earn him some serious coin, but Deadsy had flipped before the evening could turn to anything like rewards. All in all, he would have been left with nothing. Except … He slipped into the booth opposite Willow and smiled. "Long night, huh? So what do you think, lot of character in here …?"

She was watching one of her spiders spin in a small pool of ale. "It's what you get at a crossroads," she muttered. "All things collide." She smiled up at him. "But, yes, character. The place is creeping with it."

He smiled back. A woman nursing a pipe between two tusks brought them their drinks and a small platter of meats and cheeses. She sneered, then left them alone. Famished, Sixpence grabbed at the food.

Willow made some quick gestures to her spiders, and they all hurried off.

"Where are they off to?" Sixpence asked through a mouth-ful of cheese.

"They have webs to weave, food to catch."

He swallowed and shivered at the same time. An un-usual combination.

Sipping at her flagon, Willow studied their fellow travellers. She seemed curious and intrigued by everyone she saw.

Sixpence looked around. He recognized one face. Thaddeus Rattler was sitting in a nest of shadows, marking time by hustling any fool that stopped too long at his table. A hollowed man was standing by a window, peering out. His ragged cloak seemed to wave, as if beckoning to any who might pass in the night, mistaking him for another. Women in crooked hats exchanged spiky observations. "All doom and no gloom makes God dull at parties," said one, nodding at a cross on a girl's necklace.

"When did you meet your first ghost?" Willow asked Sixpence.

Her eyes pierced his, as if she saw more than she should. Perhaps she did. It was exhilarating to be seen in such a way.

"I was young—too young, really ..." The memory drifted to the surface sometimes, although he preferred those waters to be still. "I was talking to my grandfather, years after he'd gone. First they thought I was just remembering him, in my way, but then they caught me *listening* ..."

"What did he tell you?"

He fidgeted. This was all a little close. "He told me death was a tether, holding you fast. The grip loosened with time, but he said it was nice to wait it out with someone you knew."

A fine piece of web stretched between her fingers. "A tether?" she muttered. "The universe repeats the strangest, simplest shapes, over and over."

"As if we're all bound," he said, voice as quiet as hers.

She looked up at him, and he watched her unravel the words before nodding.

As though the silence were too much, she quickly looked for something to observe. "So many people going so many ways. Just crows that cross in the dark ..."

He smiled at the expression, last heard at his grandfather's knee. "You have any family?" he asked.

A tilt of her head made him feel he'd brushed a nerve. "Just spiders now," she said, eventually.

"Sorry."

She shook her head. "I made mistakes. Forsook a family trade for a road that crawled. Least that was how Mother put it."

Sixpence shot her a rueful smile. "What do they know, huh? You can't ignore where your feet want to lead you."

She looked distant. "I didn't know what was happening to me at first. When I was still a girl, there were nightmares, endless voices and thoughts that weren't mine … I woke one night, and a spider was weaving a dream catcher above me. It was trying to connect, to communicate. It was only then I understood what the dreams were, what I was hearing. That spider was the first that spoke to me. It wanted to help. I learned all I could until Father came in one day and panicked. Took one look at the spider, and me nodding away to words he couldn't hear, and just ground it under a boot." She flinched at the memory. "They're drawn to me, come out of hiding whenever I'm around. I try to look after them, protect them where I can. I *try*."

"Did the dream catcher work?"

"For a time. Now it's enough to talk and let the dreams listen."

"Better dreams, though?"

At first she was quiet, but then she nodded. A sudden tinkling of musical notes made them look across the room. A black piano was leaning against a corner, and a goblin was trying out some keys while a slender figure hunched over him. She threw back a veil and broke into a goblin melody.

Jaws across the tavern dropped. Goblins were often dismissed, being lowly or ragged in nature, but they were a revelation when they caught you off guard. People turned to find the singer, only to freeze when they discovered a crooked form that surprised them.

Sixpence leaned back and let the voice sing of a mountain far away. Some of the words were clumsy, others cruel, but the voice cradled them all nonetheless. *Within the mountain was a hall carved from stone, and creatures dancing over flames and courting with the ashes.* The goblin's tone lilted and ebbed like water coursing over rock, or blood slipping through fingers. She approached a crescendo, reaching a heartsick peak that made men judder and demons turn.

It was all that a song could be and more.

When the notes and chords finished trembling, the two goblins walked together to a quiet corner while applause broke out in uncertain pockets around the room. They sat and shared small smiles just for each other.

"And that's why I followed the road," Willow said softly. "To see the shades in the shadows."

Smiling, he wanted to show he shared the sentiment, to say something tender, but a loud comment at the door made his mouth go dry.

"Deadsy, you old bastard! What're you doing in a dive like this?"

Sixpence saw Bawd Deadsy, dishevelled and seething, in the doorway of the tavern. His gaze roamed angrily around the room, and burly henchmen glowered at each shoulder.

Sixpence remembered the shadow's warning. He'd thought the shadow was afraid Deadsy would follow it, but it had been warning *him*. Nothing stopped Deadsy from doing things his way. Nothing spoiled a good night's *fun*.

"We need to go," he whispered.

Too late.

Deadsy's gaze had ceased wandering. He pointed a gun towards their booth. "Ruiners! Fun-breakers! Party quitters!"

Deadsy barged through the tables, his minions in lumbering pursuit. Sixpence had only half slid out of the booth before Deadsy found clear space between them and brought up his gun. Willow stared at it, twitched her fingers, and her remaining spiders scuttled out of sight.

Deadsy stopped before them. "Oh my, you've been to a marvellous party, haven't you? I bet you'd never seen such a splendid buffet of violence! And yet you walked off, undead. *Ungrateful*, that's what it is."

He laughed, like the night was young and could still be saved.

Sixpence felt heavy, as if the blood in his veins had slowed, already dreaming he were dead. He tried to speak. "Hey, Deadsy—"

Deadsy's finger flicked the safety on the gun. Pursing his lips, he shook his head. "Hush now. The party's not over until the gun is sated." He glanced at Willow. One of her hands was sliding under the table. "Go on, girl, shoot me with a spider. See what happens this time."

She froze. Soon the bullets would sing. Would there be applause this time?

"Are you going to shoot us in front of everyone?"

Deadsy shrugged, glanced around, and shot a passing drunk-ard in the back. The man keeled over and hit the floor with a wet thud. Deadsy paused. "Anyone? Any feelings?"

No one in the tavern even looked at him. Either they didn't care, or Deadsy had an aura that no one wanted to tangle with. Sixpence knew it meant they were damned either way. His mind went to his ghouls, who would be separated, lost once more. Willow's spiders, disconnected, unwanted.

Deadsy looked around as if eager for someone to prove troublesome. The endless murmur of conversation had only briefly abated, and now it began building again. He looked back at Sixpence, the gun rising, the bullets waiting. Cruelty would be indulged, *justified*, for who had ever opposed it?

"Halt!"

A sudden, striking voice from the doorway made them all look. The pastor was standing in the entrance, a crowd of ghouls at his back. He pointed at Deadsy. "You devil! You have these spirits tied to a contract. Set them free at once!"

Deadsy looked appalled. "Get back to the woods, you dogs. You've a mansion to guard!"

Sixpence slid out of the booth, horrified. "You think you *own* them?"

Deadsy looked irritated. "They sold their souls to my ancestors. Fools."

The pastor stood to his full height, shining with green energy and brimming with righteous anger. "Villain! Cur! This will not stand! Release them at once, or face judgement!"

Deadsy laughed, because everything amused Deadsy. The laugh died when he realized it had replaced all the sound in the room. The tavern had fallen abruptly silent. People were staring. Some began whispering.

He'd crossed a line.

"The Deadsys. Bastards, all of them."

"Who d'you think he's got in them woods?"

"My nan, we buried her whole, but it weren't right. There was an *absence* to her ..."

Sixpence pointed at Deadsy. "He can release them at any time, but he won't." He raised his voice. "That's the Deadsy way: throw a party, and kill who turns up! Imagine what he does when he finds someone's left him a bunch of souls."

"Put 'em to work," Deadsy muttered. "What else?"

The mood shifted quickly. People stood up from their tables. Deadsy paled. "Uh ..."

"Just release them," Sixpence suggested, "and leave."

Pointing at Deadsy, Willow added, "And go where no spider can see you."

He licked his lips. "Well, what do I care, eh? Just *souls*."

The ghouls quivered in anticipation.

Hesitating, Deadsy looked around. The gun began trembling in his grip. Bloodlust had made him wander too far, and he had no friends here.

"Watch the one on his left."

Sixpence shivered. The shadow was still with him. He looked at the henchman on Deadsy's left just in time to see a knife appear in his hand. The blade cut through the air between them, and Sixpence ducked as it flew over his head.

The second the knife hit a wall, the tension broke. Thaddeus Rattler, who'd been creeping closer, brought a bottle down on the henchman's head. The man hit the floor hard.

Sixpence tensed. He felt the shadow leap out of him and dive into Deadsy.

"What was —" Deadsy's eyes shot wide.

The second henchman went down, grunting, as a chair crowned

him. Rattler, member of the guild of gentlemen thieves, gave Sixpence a curt nod. Many of his colleagues had checked in with Sixpence over the years. Ghosts came in handy on the oddest of jobs, apparently.

Deadsy staggered back a step. His eyes were rolling in his head. "The contracts are void," he hissed.

"All of them?" Sixpence nudged.

"*All* of them."

Released from their bonds, the ghouls began shining, as if smudged fingerprints on their souls were being wiped free. As one, they turned to glower at Deadsy, who seemed to suddenly realize he was at their mercy. "You know, I think there's a party over at Grave Hills. If I leave now, I might just make it—"

The pastor pointed at him. "Callous fiend!"

Deadsy dropped his gun and dived out an open window. The ghouls raced straight through the tavern's walls and chased after him into the night.

Sixpence turned to the pastor and raised an eyebrow.

"Met those fellows in the woods," the ghoul explained. "Quite lost they were, grabbing people off the road in Deadsy's name. I was giving them a proper talking to when I saw that awful ruffian walk by. Knew he was up to no good and heading your way, so I rallied them into action."

"I'm glad you did."

The pastor looked around, taking in the tavern, then the wall the ghouls had left through. "Might stay a while, tell them their options."

Sixpence grinned. "You do that." Still smiling, he sat back with Willow, and they fell into easy silence while spiders and ghouls pulled up and spun seats nearby.

"How about you? Will you stay for a few drinks?" he asked.

"And then the road?"

He nodded. "Perhaps ... Do you think we might be going the same way?"

She considered, then her lips parted with a slight smile. "You should be careful. I want to weave a great dream catcher that will release everyone and everything from every fear. Some won't like that."

"Well, I aim to walk with the dead while they have nowhere to go. Should be an odd road."

"Do you promise?"

He smiled. With that, they drank until the sun rose upon tendrils of mist, which linked hands across the land, dreamily weaving the beginnings of another day.

An idle thought, but one that made the web dance.

THE 2024 MAGPIE AWARD FOR POETRY

THE 2024 MAGPIE AWARD FOR POETRY

We're delighted to present the winning poem and runners-up of the 2024 Magpie Award for Poetry, with commentary from final judge Renée Sarojini Saklikar. Here's what Renée had to say about these amazing poems:

Winner: **'From the back row of the theatre of I Am' by Angela Rebrec:** *"Intelligence and a sad-funny wit combine with a narrative form that pulls us in and resonates with unsettling images. The final well-crafted stanza shocks and haunts in equal measure. I kept returning to this one!"*

First Runner-Up: **'HAVE YOU SEEN PRECIOUS?' by Cicely Grace:** *"[A] strong personal voice, expanding our sense of what a poem can do in the department of story-telling. I loved all the word-filled sentences, the depth and density. A hybrid of lyric prose and the prose poem. Refreshing to see the line subsumed into the sentence. Lots of possibilities of form."*

Second Runner-Up: **'Roving Писанки' by Veronika Gorlova:** *"In our cultural moment, fractured by war and humanitarian disasters, situated in a climate emergency, the combination of surreal imagery and words other than English, with a precise diction and stanza shape, intrigues and provokes. . . . Brave for the poet to just let the two languages cohere."*

Congratulations to 2024's winners, and thanks to all who submitted to this contest! And our thanks again to final judge Renée Sarojini Saklikar, renowned author of *Bramah and The Beggar*

Boy and *Brahmah's Quest*, as well as 'Man With Golden Helmet' and 'Told under the Linden Tree' in *Pulp Literature* issues 28 and 37. Our gratitude as well to poets Emily Osborne and Daniel Cowper, our *Pulp Literature* poetry editors and first judges. Their books *Safety Razor* and *Grotesque Tenderness* are wonderful and intriguing reads.

Angela Rebrec *is a Hellenic-Canadian who lives and works on the unceded lands of the Kwantlen, Tsawwassen, and Musqueam peoples. A multidisciplinary artist, her poetry films have been recognized at film festivals including the Filmmaker Life Awards. Angela's 2020 collaboration with composer Mickie Wadsworth for ART SONG LAB has been included in the first volume of NewMusicShelf's* Anthology of New Music: Trans & Nonbinary Voices, Vol. 1. *She is the founding and current president of the Delta Literary Arts Society. Her poem 'On a Dark Lake's Edge' appeared in Pulp Literature issue 18, Spring 2018.*

Cicely Grace *is a writer based in Vancouver, BC. She holds a degree in English literature from UBC, where she specialized in twentieth-century women's writing, modernism, gender, and sexuality. Her work has been featured in* The Garden Statuary, The Foundationalist, *and* Contemporary Verse 2. *She was the second-place recipient of the 2023 Foster Poetry Prize.*

Veronika Gorlova *is a queer, autistic, Jewish poet and writer living on the unceded territories of the Musqueam, Squamish, and Tsleil-Waututh people, also known as Vancouver. Her family immigrated to Canada from Ukraine when she was five years old, and she has lived in many parts of the country. Her writing appears in* Arc Poetry Magazine, the /tɛmz/ Review, Cathexis Northwest Press *and* Poetry Pause, *among others.*

From the back row of the theatre of I Am

by Angela Rebrec

Allow yourself the use of assonance — but do not give it up as an offering. 'What's mine is mine.' Collect your thoughts, organize them according to weight, in which chapter they first appeared, alto or soprano, or if they swear like a trucker. Place them into their proper drawers. Use labels if you must.

When I was five my father held me upside down by my ankles hoping the penny I had swallowed would come out. Mind your Ps and Qs but defend your vowels with your life. Even David prayed for the Lord to set a guard over his mouth.

Sit cross-legged in the experimental film of your life. Ad-lib with a voice that reeks of popcorn with real butter. The first films ever made read like the opening verses of Genesis: a walking man; a nude woman. In which I cannot confirm any of this is fact.

'I am' is the shortest complete sentence in the English language. The slow motion slap my father gave me after my dinner plate smashed to the floor. Some facts remain facts while others merely opinions of facts. Even the most hardened critic will not immediately see what is happening on the screen.

In the structure of Greek tragedy the actors wore masks. In the structure of Greek tragedy the actors were always men. In the structure of Greek tragedy the chorus wrapped up the play with a processional song offering morals and wisdom the male audience was expected to take home to their women.

Run the screen test of King David in which he recites the lines *Let a righteous man strike you — it is a kindness.* Now add a rating. Add two thumbs up. Way up.

Consonant articulation involves substantial constriction in the vocal tract. My children watched from the front row as my husband choked me in glorious 3D and THX surround sound. Louder than a monologue, than a prayer, than all the facts added together. I am. Projected to the last row.

$\mathcal{H}$AVE YOU SEEN PRECIOUS?

BY CICELY GRACE

A rain-blurred sign says HAVE YOU SEEN PRECIOUS?
the image of the kitten long obscured in pools of bleeding
ink. I walk past three more copies tacked to three more
telephone poles, all of them ravaged by rain. Precious was last seen
in October. It is now April, the season for tending,
and I've decided to deal with myself. So I'm climbing carpeted stairs
to somewhere I've never been, a little office off Arbutus.
A green sign tells me to take off my shoes and I am ashamed
of the smell. A whole winter's leaking is alive in the lining.
I have the sniffles.

The therapist is kind like the website promised. Her lips are precisely
pink. She asks why I keep looking at my hands. What is the most efficient
way to say this: They are something that I am sure of. I hope she can tell
this is hard for me. I tell her that it's hard being beautiful, what it has done
to men and to my mother. And I speak fondly of my pain,
that precious weapon, how I feel that I am weak and have little else
to wield. I am relieved to hear my symptoms are very common

for girls like me. Eventually she has to say, would you like me to charge
the card on file? I take her advice: I shall create a vocabulary
for the things I see and feel.

I go to the grocery store to buy fish and oranges, an $8.50 bag
of squash soup. It is still morning and the bell peppers are untouched
in their even rows. I've spent the early hours thinking of myself
as a daughter and a lover, a victim and a bitch. How peaceful
to now just be a woman buying groceries, and naming the things
that are certain: There is the cashier giving me the paper bag,
there are my hands clasped beneath it. I walk home like an old lady,
slowly and alone, admiring the patience
of some stranger who despite all the morning's mist has their laundry
pinned on a taut wire. There is the congregation of old men
outside the McDonald's with their coffee cups and simple wisdoms,
    great men
of the world, who have long quit searching for things that cannot be
    remembered
during a cigarette, or read in the morning's paper, who have finished grieving
all of the things that were precious and lost. Two more things I know:
There is a fallen nest beneath a tree, pathetically empty, a waste of weaving.
And there is a toddler who climbs the steps to his porch on all fours.

Roving Писанки

by Veronika Gorlova

I have an egg with магической силой
    and the fate of the land depends
        on the tenderness of my hands.

It is one of several in my meadows
    guarding the gates to this земле.

I used to have more but a witch came through and cast
    a storm. Lightning shattered them to pieces,
      left me бессильной.

After it was over I gathered all the fragments,
    ground them down to снег
    and sprinkled them into the реку.

Now there are only a few, and they appear
    in неудобных местах.

Once, strolling through the tall grasses
        the bottom of my foot felt something гладкое.
            I froze, bent down and moved the писанка
                out of harm's way.

Another time, lying in the field with my lover
        руки, ноги, языки intertwined, I rolled over
            and felt an oval along my spine.

I pushed her away, scooped it up, and cradled it gently in my hand.
        She didn't understand. I'm the only one who
            может их видеть.

Last week, having lunch with a friend, I saw one
        плавающий in the middle of her bowl,
            like a glacier in a болото.

I swapped our soups, carefully guided my spoon around the сфера
        so it wouldn't precipitate a calving.

I've been trying to keep them in a корзина on the kitchen counter
        but их силы выросли. Every morning the basket lies bare.
            They're constantly shifting. Они напуганы.

I'm making more but it takes time, it takes breath,
        it takes кровь. Meanwhile the grass turns
            желтой, the fields are затоплены,
                the land is losing

                терпение.

Today, my hands weren't steady enough. Bright eggshell
развалилось на части, onto my lap. I collected
the fragments in a mortar, made kaleidoscopic сахар
and stirred it into my tea.

For the rest of the day I sat by the window and cried
for the meadows, drank my potion to отогнать ведьм.
The brew turned salty, горькой,
undrinkable.

I watched a cloud start to form
in the неразборчивом sky.

BAD BACKUP

Gabriel Craven & Mikayla Fawcett

Gabriel Craven *is a comic artist and writer from Steveston, BC. His love of pulpy genre fiction runs hand in hand with his focus on small stories and everyday experiences.*

Mikayla Fawcett *is an interdisciplinary writer and artist. Before they finished typing this sentence, they went for a wetland wander, and then added three more buckets of yuck to the zombies featured in this comic.*

FINAL RESTORATION
BAD BACKUP

SO.
I AM ON SITE.
WHERE ARE YOU?
SORRY, SERGE!!
GOT CAUGHT IN A HEALTH CHECK-POINT!
LINE'S NOT TOO LONG!
SHOULD BE ON MY WAY IN THE NEXT TEN.
IT'S FINE.
I WILL UNLOAD ALL THE EQUIPMENT MYSELF, YES?
FINAL RESTORATION
FR
JUST CHILL AND HAVE A SMOKE, DUDE.
FINAL RESTORATION
I'LL BE THERE SOON.
YOU'RE ON LIGHT DUTIES, RIGHT?
DON'T HURT YOURSELF UNLOADING ON YOUR OWN, BUD.

"SO SORRY, SERGEI!"
"JUST CHILL."
"HAVE A SMOKE."

DON'T HURT YOURSELF, DUUUDE!

MAYBE GET TO JOB SITE ON TIME--
MAYBE THEN I CAN "JUST CHILL."

MAYBE DON'T USE MY BACK AS EXCUSE TO SLACK OFF--!

GLUHHH!
HHAA AAAAUUUGH!
RRUH
AAAAUUGH!!
FR
DriHeave
NNGUH
MMUHRK
HHHHRRROODA
AGHHHAAOOOURRAAU

UUUHHHRRR
HFF--
OOOAAGHH
HFF--
AUUUUGHHH
HFF--
RAAUUU
UGH, RIGHT. ZOMBIES.
HFF--
AT LEAST SOMEBODY COMES WHEN I CALL.
WHAT CAN I DO FOR YOU, SIR?
HFF-- WHAT'S THAT?
YOU WANT TO HELP ME MOVE THE E.G.?
UUUAAAAAAHHH
GHAAA!
HHRRRRHHOAA
OH NO? YOU JUST WANT TO EAT ME FOR LUNCH?
WELL, THEN.
LET'S SEE YOU KEEP UP WITH SERGEI.

HEH
HRM
HUP!
ACK!
EUGH

TCH!
HELLO GREG.
WHERE THE HECK ARE YOU?
I TOLD YOU, I HADTA GO THROUGH A CHECK-POINT.
SO YOU ARE CLOSE NOW?
YEAH! I'M TOTALLY ON THE WAY.
BE LIKE... I DUNNO, TEN MINUTES?
ARE YOU JOKING WITH ME?!
I AM BEING CHASED AND NO THANKS TO YOU MY BACK IS BROKE!
OH DUDE
YOU DIDN'T TRY 'N' MOVE THAT DE-HUM DID YOU?
FINAL RESTORATION
FINAL RESTORATION

OK!
GOTTA GO.
ZOMBIES ARE HERE.
WHEN YOUR SLOW ASS GETS HERE
I HOPE MY ZOMBIE CORPSE TAKES A BITE OUT OF YOU!
GLAU!
LET'S GET TO WORK!
GLAAIGH!
BASH!
ACKHH!

HHNG!
...OKAY.
FINE.
ALRIGHT, EVERYBODY.
LINE UP AND TAKE A BITE.
HHHAAGHH
GRRUHH

JUST LEAVE ENOUGH OF ME TO GET BACK UP.
HONK!

FINAL RESTORATION

YOU JUST ABOUT RAN ME OVER.
FINAL·RESTORATION
GET IN, YOU MELODRAMATIC JERK!

C'MON, MAN!
HURRY IT UP!

thmp
thmp
FINAL·RESTORATION

OK, GREG.
YOU MIGHT BE LATE, BUT I MUST ADMIT,
YOU GOT HERE IN TIME TO SAVE ME, SO...
THANK YOU.

NO PROBS, DUDE!
EVEN GOT A CUPPA COFFEE FOR YA!
FINAL·RESTOR
HOT! CHAUD!

THANKS
WAIT.
YOU STOPPED FOR COFFEE?
YEAH, BUD! PICKED IT UP ON THE WAY OVER!
FINAL-RESTORATION

AFTER I CALLED YOU THE FIRST TIME, YOU STILL STOPPED FOR COFFEE?!
FINAL · RESTORATION
YEAH?
YOU SOUNDED LIKE YOU NEEDED A COFFEE, MAN!

I NEEDED HELP, NOT COFFEE!!
SERGEI. BUD.
THIS IS WHAT I WAS TALKING ABOUT.
YOU GOTTA LEARN TO CHILL.
FINAL RESTORATION
Fin!

THE SHEPHERDESS: NARBONNE

J M Landels

JM Landels is torn between travelling the world to teach writing and swordfighting, and never leaving her idyllic farm in Langley, BC. Her debut series, fantasy bestseller Allaigna's Song: Overture, and the sequels, Aria and Chorale, are available from Pulp Literature Press and most booksellers. You can follow her adventures with pen and sword at jmlandels.stiffbunnies.com.

The Shepherdess: Narbonne

Previously …

Toinette Berger is a shepherdess-turned-spy and a member of the mysterious Order of the Silver Branch. She has spent the last year of her apprenticeship at La Tectume, a refuge belonging to the Order and hidden in a seemingly abandoned château-fort in the low Pyrenées. This period of rest comes to an end with the arrival of a face from the past: the courtier Michel la Foix, who arrives to entreat the help of Toinette's mistress, Madame la Comtesse, on behalf of an acquaintance known only as James.

Since I'd set foot inside castle Tectume, I had seldom ventured down the mountainside. All memory of riding had disappeared from my body, and sitting Marteau's lumpy gait was punishing my bottom before we even reached the valley. The air felt dense and rich down here, and the skiff of snow that had frosted the roofs of the château this morning was nothing but a damp memory.

"Remind me again why we couldn't take a carriage?" I asked the men on either side of me.

"Because the joy of mounting a horse is second only to that of a lover in your arms," announced Michel.

"Speak for yourself," grumbled Henri. "There are many things, I find, that rank in between those two. A glass of brandy, for instance, and a padded chair inside a sedan."

"I agree with Henri for once," I said, shifting my seat bones. "Surely we could have taken the carriage as far as Narbonne and sent it back with Gwyn?"

"Not as swiftly, nor as quietly, as we can thus," said Madame, twisting in her saddle to look at us from three horse-lengths ahead. "And, speaking of speed, we need to put some on." She put her heels to her horse, who picked up a brisk trot. I groaned, and asked the same of Marteau, envying Luc who trailed behind us. Babette's cart was unsprung, but at least Luc, perched high upon bundles of clothing, could shift his seat at will.

Three days later in a tawdry inn on Narbonne's rue Cabriol, the three men and I drank flat, watered beer beside a hearth more filled with smoke than fire. We had arrived nearly two hours before, and conversation had died off early. Henri leaned against the wall, his eyes closed, while Michel stood frequently, walked around our knot of chairs, and sat again. This disturbed my adopted hound, Jacques, who rose and circled my chair each time. And I calmed him each time with scratches behind his grizzled ears.

If the other patrons of the tavern were disturbed by this behaviour, they showed no sign. My own eyes began to droop, until Jacques snapped them open with a bark. I twisted to see a tall man standing behind me.

"Milady," he said to me, though I was still dressed in men's clothing. "Your mistress has need of you."

The ceiling of the upper floor was so low that even I felt I might hit my head on the ancient beams. I knocked on the crooked wooden door, and when there was no answer, I pushed it open, wincing as it scraped along the floor.

Madame had told us little to nothing of why she had agreed to meet this James, nor what the meeting entailed. She had said she would be exhausted afterwards, but I wasn't prepared for the sight before me. The dozens of candles which had been placed around the room had guttered or been blown out, and the only light was the dim grey of a January afternoon that crept in through the missing slats of the shutters.

Madame lay face down on the bed, her limbs tangled in the twisted sheets, her damp hair plastered to her back and looking for all the world like rivers of old blood. I tiptoed over, loath to wake her if I didn't need to. I picked up her wrist and felt the weak pulse. It was at least steady.

I unwrapped the sheets from her legs, noticed actual blood and hoped it was just her courses. She didn't stir as I arranged her limbs and brought the sheet over her clammy back.

The water in the cracked pitcher by the window was cold, but there was no hearth, so it would have to do. I poured a measure into the steel cup I carried in my bag, then added two drops of tincture and a drop of oil. Dipping a clean cloth in the cup, I began to wash her, starting with her sweaty brow, her ear, the back of her neck. She wore nothing but the ruby necklace I had carried to her all the way from Paris the prior spring. I lifted the sheet in portions, washing one limb, then covering it again to keep her warm. I rolled her over, cradling her head, and began again at her face. My fingers were both burning and numb from the solution, but I continued until every inch of her skin had been wiped clean.

Then I washed my hands, shaking them to bring back feeling, and sat down to wait some more. I considered sending word down to Henri, Luc, and Michel, who would be wondering what had kept us, but I would not expose any hint of Madame's vulnerability to them. As the day darkened, I relit candles and paced the room in between checking Madame's breath and pulse, rubbing her feet to bring them warmth, and pointlessly rearranging our possessions. She had said we would travel the next morning, but I had my doubts.

I longed to remove the necklace, which seemed colder by far than Madame's skin, and put it safely away in its pouch, but she had forbidden that. Instead I took out my piece of black glass. It was not a polished lens like the one in the lorgnette of Grandmère Paris, but merely an irregular shard worn smooth on the edges. It could not focus and decipher alchemical workings the way Grandmère's could, but it could still show their bluish glow, if in a blurry and imprecise manner. I rubbed it with the piece of chamois leather I kept it wrapped in, and held it to my eye.

At first all was dark, despite the many candles in the room, but then a foggy blue smear appeared: the line of the rubies strung about Madame's neck. I had examined that necklace a dozen times at least on my journey from Paris to la Tectume, and seen no trace of alchemy upon it till now.

But it was not just the rubies. Faint blue lines, like the veins in Madame's porcelain skin, tracked their way outward from the necklace. With each breath she took, the lines pulsed a little brighter, and faded with each exhale.

Was the necklace draining her of strength, or imbuing her with it? When we had arrived at this inn at noon, we'd taken a different room in order for her to change from her riding clothes. I'd helped her into the morning robe that now lay folded beneath me on the chair, and I'd fastened the rubies about her neck. It would have been odd attire anywhere, and was entirely out of place in this shoddy inn.

"When I am done, Toinette," she had said, "I will need to sleep, perhaps till tomorrow morning. Whatever you do, do not remove these." She touched the array of rubies at her throat. "Use the tincture and the oil if you think they're needed, but otherwise, let me rest."

Loath as I was to leave her, I made my way downstairs to inform the men that we'd be spending the night here. "Where is Michel?" I asked Luc and Henri.

"Gone with his friend," replied the former.

"What did you expect from the little shit?" added the latter.

I shrugged. I had no space in my thoughts to ponder Michel or the man who had left Madame in her state. I took her belongings from the other room, leaving it for Luc and Henri to share—though I had no doubt Henri would bully Luc into sleeping in the stable to keep watch on Babette and the horses. Were my heart not so full of Madame, I may have interceded on Luc's behalf. But an eye on the horses was not a bad idea in so rough a quarter, so I held my peace.

I stayed awake through the night, with a single candle burning so I could watch Madame's breath rise and fall. The room lacked a hearth, being heated by the inn's main fire below, which I suspected was allowed to go out by midnight. I pulled my woollen skirt over my breeches and tied on my apron for warmth. I alternated between pacing the creaking floorboards and creeping under the covers—clothes, cloak, and all—to share my warmth with Madame. During the latter spells, I kept my eyes open by biting my lips and digging my fingernails into my palms so as not to succumb to sleep. I invited Jacques onto the bed as well, it being January and the fleas all dead.

When grey light found its way through gaps in the shutters, I heard sounds of movement in the kitchen below. I made one last check of the unchanged pulse in Madame's pale wrist and blew out the last of the candles.

"Stay," I said to Jacques, who made to get off the bed. "Keep her warm."

He whined, but put his head back on his paws and watched me slip out of the room.

Unwilling to wait for the morning bread to bake, I begged an end of yesterday's loaf, along with a measure of passable wine.

When I returned with this meagre breakfast, I was greeted at the door by Jacques, who was enthusiastically thumping his tail against the leg of the bed.

"Jacques!" I remonstrated. "I told you to stay on the bed."

"That's my fault, chérie," came the most welcome voice in the world. "I tumbled him off so I could sit up." Madame was sitting on the edge of the bed, wrapped in her morning robe.

"Madame." I dropped onto the bed beside her, embracing her with wine in one hand and bread in the other. "I have been so worried."

She kissed me on the forehead. "Thank you for your vigil. There's no one I'd trust more." She extracted the wine from my hand. "Is this for me?"

"I've ordered a proper breakfast for you, but it may be a while," I said.

"Then help me get dressed, and we'll share it downstairs." She tore off a piece of bread to dip in the wine. "This will sustain me till then."

After a hasty toilette in the dim room and a mouthful of stale bread for each of us, including Jacques, we made our way downstairs. For all her casual demeanour, Madame's steps wobbled on the stairs, and she braced with both arms against the close walls.

She had taken off the rubies and put them in their chamois pouch. "My strength is restored enough," she insisted, "and they attract far too much attention." She tucked them into her pocket and shifted the band so it hid beneath the fullest part of her riding skirt.

I settled her beside the new fire to wait for fresh bread, warm wine, and cold meats.

"Bread is enough," she insisted to the landlord, but I overruled her and asked him to bring some of last night's bean and sausage stew, warmed up, as well as cheese, butter, and whatever confiture was in the pantry. Madame's normally slim form seemed wasted today. Her shoulders and arms were stick-like, and the edges of her stays had nearly met when I laced her up.

She sank against the back of the chair and closed her eyes. "I suppose it is too much to hope for a demitasse of coffee?"

I shook my head. "I doubt they have it here. But when we rode through the main street yesterday, I smelled it. There may be a Turkish vendor there. I could send Luc to find out."

She opened her eyes, which seemed larger in her gaunt face. "That would be heavenly, my dear."

After my nightlong watch, I was uneasy leaving her alone. I dashed upstairs and pounded on Henri's door until I heard a groan of agreement at the suggestion he relocate his sorry corpse downstairs, and then I went to the stables to rouse Luc.

Luc was up already, currying Madame's mount. The bay stallion had liberated itself from Sauvegarde's retinue when I'd set fire to the inn near la Tectume the year before. Madame had insisted I give the little stallion a name, since he had attached himself to my growing collection of beasts: Marteau, Jacques, and Henri and Luc if you counted men. I felt Marteau's name, given after I first had to withstand his trot, was unkind and perhaps too prophetic. I had no particular fondness for this new horse, which was far too lifey for me to ride. But he was affectionate, and had a kind eye and sweet nose. Madame said he was most likely bred from the desert stock of northern Africa, so I named him Habibi, a word from Dr Ahmed's tongue, which meant 'beloved'.

Despite the cold winter, he'd grown hardly any coat — unlike Marteau, Babette, and Henri's great Norman horse Mangetout, who were all as woolly as baudets de Poitou. In the summer, his coat gleamed a gold-tinged dappled bronze, but now, in the winter, it was a velvety red.

"Luc," I said, startling lad and stallion both. "I applaud your industry, but it will be some time before we ride."

"Mademoiselle!" Luc said, giving Habibi, who had shied into him, a shove back to the centre of the stall. Once the stallion was where he should be, Luc touched the dandy brush to his wool cap and gave a bow, his other hand on Habibi's shoulder to steady him. "How is your mistress?"

"Better than last night, but nowhere near ready to depart. She has asked for coffee." I ignored Luc's puzzled look. "I smelled coffee when we rode in yesterday. Not too far." I have an excellent sense of direction, and an even better memory — which may be why I have survived as long as I have — and so was able to give him precise directions.

"But the horses—" he protested.

"I roused Henri to take over from you," I interrupted, hoping the man was already moving. "Go. The sooner you get back, the sooner we can be on our way."

Despite my assurance to Luc, I was by no means easy leaving the animals and Babette's cart unattended. I sent furious thoughts in Henri's direction, as if by thinking I could rouse the man, and told myself that Madame was well enough by the fire with food coming soon.

The sounds of morning were already eking into the stable yard. The shouts of a drover and the unmistakable smell of a herd of goats wafted in, followed by the barks of dogs, the rumble of an oxcart, and the pleasant morning greetings of denizens throwing open their shutters despite the chilly wind.

And then I heard a four-horse carriage rattle and clop up the cobbles, and the driver call a halt. A carriage in this part of town, at this hour of the morning, was odd. And carriages almost always bore me bad luck.

I hurried back through the connecting door from the stable to the inn room in time to see the hem of Madame's cloak disappear through the door to the street. I dashed across the room, dodging tables and benches, and stumbled over a footstool near the door.

"Madame!" I called, as a liveried footman handed her by the elbow into the carriage.

She looked over her shoulder and cast an indifferent eye on me. "My servants will pay the bill, mademoiselle." She waved a languid hand towards the upstairs chamber, where Henri still slept, curling her fingers in a motion that signalled *follow*. To avoid the sweep of her cloak, the footman moved backwards, revealing the sheen of steel in his hand: a blade no bigger than a demi-pied, but long enough.

Madame stepped into the carriage, and a hand pulled down the blind with a snap. I could see Madame's face just long enough to catch the subtle shake of her head and her lips mouthing the word *non*.

I lost precious moments, flummoxed by my ignorance of what had just happened. Madame's lips had told me not to follow, but the hand she had waved signalled the opposite. Did she mean Henri should follow and I should stay? Did he know something I did not?

I stepped into the street as the carriage moved off, and bellowed at the closed shutters of the upper storey. "Henri, damn you! Are you up yet?"

A muffled curse accompanied the clatter of wood as Henri threw back a shutter and stuck his head out. In his hand he held a razor, and his face was half-covered in soap. "Can a man not finish shaving in peace?"

I gestured down the street. "Madame has been taken. In a carriage. At knife point—I think." There would be no profit in asking Henri to follow, half-dressed and half-shaven as he was. "I'm taking Marteau after her." I dashed back to the stable yard, blessing Luc for his serendipitous impatience to tack the horses so early.

Hurried as I was, I still took the time to warm Marteau's icy-cold bit beneath my apron. My numb fingers fumbled at the buckles on his bridle, and by the time I led him out of the yard and clambered onto his back, at least a half-dozen minutes had passed. The carriage was long gone, but I set off in its direction, over the Pont des Marchands.

The bridge was now so crowded with merchants opening their shops and parking their carts for the day that I had to slow Marteau to a trot to navigate it. I hoped the carriage had had even more difficulty.

"Excusez-moi, madame," I asked of a woman setting out pies at the far end. "Have you seen a coach and four drive past?"

The woman scowled at me. "If you're not buying a *tarte*, move your beast." She made a rude gesture at Marteau, who, agitated by the increasing bustle and my own nerves, left a splatter of overly wet manure in front of her stall.

I called out over the heads of the merchants. "Anyone? Anyone at all see a carriage?"

I felt a tug at the hem of my skirt and looked down to find a girl of seven or thereabouts holding my stirrup.

"I saw it, madame. Are you riding astride?"

I ignored the impertinent question. "Which way?"

"Give me a ride and I'll show you."

I stared at the ragged thing gripping my stirrup iron while I contemplated how much her information was worth. But since no one else had answered my call, I shifted my purse behind my hip, leaned over, and lifted her by the arms onto the front of my saddle. She smelled of goats — to me, an odour less offensive than that of most perfumed courtiers — and was as skinny as a plucked sparrow. I welcomed the warmth of her body in front of me, for I had left my cloak on a chair at the inn, but I kept an eye on her hands and a feel for the purse at my back.

One of those small, grubby hands clenched the pommel, and the other pointed ahead and right. "That way."

"Are you sure?" I asked. It was a narrow street, and would be a hard turn for a four-horse carriage.

"Of course! But you'd better hurry; it was a long time ago now."

Could a child so young have mischief in her heart? Of course she could. I remembered my sisters with a sudden longing, and kicked Marteau into his awful trot. The girl let out a scream and giggle mixed, and I had to wrap an arm around her to keep her from bouncing off the saddle.

Several thoughts bounced in my head in time with the laughing girl, chief among them that this urchin was leading me into an ambush. But that would mean she had foreknowledge of my pursuit, for what sort of ambush waited on a stranger to arrive and ask directions? Or was she working for Madame? Or her abductor? For the hundredth time or more since I'd been in Madame's service, I cursed my ignorance—not only of why Madame had suddenly been taken, or what alchemy she had performed to leave her so debilitated, but of the larger wheels and cogs that seemed to turn around her. The giggling *fille* in front of me was just one more source of uncertainty.

We hurtled down the curving street till the girl pointed at yet another turning. "That way."

I pulled Marteau to a stumbling halt on the rough cobbles. "How do you know?" From the market square, there was no way she could have seen the carriage past its first turn.

The girl twisted in the saddle to peer up at me. "Because the carriage belongs there."

With no other option but to believe her, I turned Marteau's head again. But if I was going to trust the girl this much, I would also avail myself of her local knowledge. "Whose carriage is it?" I asked.

"Dunno," she said. "Came into the city Saturday last, the grey horses all pink to their bellies from mud."

"Just the four greys pulling the carriage? Any others?" It was clear the girl was more interested in the horses than anything else.

"Two bays tied behind. And a yellow one, ridden by a soldier."

"What did the soldier look like? Was he wearing a tabard?" I asked, hoping for some insignia that would link him to a master.

She shrugged. "He didn't ride well. A bit like you. What's a tabard?"

I couldn't afford to be irritated by her insult, or to question why a goat girl had opinions on equitation. "Like your apron"—I plucked at the brown linen—"but colourful. With pictures on it."

She thought a moment. "Blue," she said, "with a yellow beast standing on its hind legs."

I didn't know enough heraldry to speculate on whose insignia it might be, but I tucked the information into the back of my mind for later as we rode past a courtyard entrance. The gate was still open and indeed the carriage was in the yard. The carriage doors were open and there appeared to be no one inside. The driver and footman, who were putting nosebags on the horses, didn't look up as we passed.

Once out of view of the courtyard, I slid off Marteau. I didn't trust the horse-mad goat girl, but perhaps I could bribe her.

"Do you know how to ride?" I asked.

"Bien sûr!" She sounded indignant. "I ride our donkey to market thrice a week."

Marteau was a good deal bigger than a donkey, but not too different in temperament.

"I have a marvellous stallion from Arabia. Would you like to see him? And perhaps sit on his back?"

She couldn't keep the sparkle out of her dark eyes as she answered, "P'rhaps."

The inn we had stayed at did not have a name. "Do you know the inn with the peeling blue shutters on the rue Cabriol?" I asked.

"The one with the crooked door? And the livery on the corner?" Trust her to know it by its stable.

I reached beneath my apron and pulled out a liard that I pressed into her hand. "I will turn that into three sols if you do what I ask. Now listen: ride to the inn and find the man Henri. You can't miss him. He's very large in height and girth, and has darker skin than I, and a curly beard. Tell him where I am."

"And what about the stallion?"

"Wait at the inn, and when we return you shall meet him."

I watched the tiny girl ride off with my horse: he was there, and then not. He was worth far more than the three sols I'd promised her, but the punishment for horse theft is harsh, and I hoped the light in her eye at the promise of the stallion would hold her to her word. I had not even asked her name, nor given her mine.

I edged back to the yard entrance and peered around the corner. A groom was bringing buckets of water to the horses, who were still hitched to the carriage, ready to travel again soon. But to return Madame or take her elsewhere? I thought of the knife that had been held to her side and decided not to wait.

The morning sun had broken through grey dawn and cast slanting shadows over half the yard. I skirted the northeast side, where the shadows were deepest, blending into the grey stone in my grey workaday garb. I kept the carriage between the groom and me and wove past bare olive trees and grapevines till I was able to approach the right side of the carriage.

It was empty, but on the ground near the front wheel was a tuft of yellow silk—a frayed bundle of fuzz from one of the ribbons in Madame's sleeve. I glanced around for another marker, keeping one eye on the groom's feet moving around the horses.

There was a cistern in the corner of the yard with a pair of overturned buckets beside it. I pulled my cap further over my face and kept my head down as I strode forwards. I dipped a bucket in the ice-rimmed cistern and walked through the doors nearest the carriage as if I worked there.

I had to pause inside to allow my eyes to adjust from the bright January sun to the unlit passage. The sounds and smells of cooking came from the right, so I put my bucket down in front of the partly open door. Let some maid benefit from a saved trip to the cistern. As my eyes became accustomed, I searched for any more telltale yellow. At last I saw it—a tiny pebble, no bigger than a peppercorn, painted yellow. Madame kept a supply of these in her pockets, as did I. It was at the end of the passage by a narrow door, and had been brushed into the crack of the stone step, no doubt by the passage of her skirts.

I eased the handle of the door and it opened with a creak that I hoped was covered by the kitchen noise. It led onto a narrow stair lit only by a casement window halfway up. I slid myself through sideways and closed the door behind me.

At the top of the stair was another closed door, and on the landing was a white handkerchief that I knew well. I picked it up by the tatted edge and saw, in the light from the casement below me, a single drop of blood, dead centre. The blood was fresh, and by its placement at the crux of the ironed folds of the handkerchief, deliberate. Unlike yellow that showed the path, red meant *stop, warning, do not go this way.*

The stairs were stone and didn't creak as I stood upon the top step. I put my ear to the wooden door. Though it was thick, it was also old, with cracks between the oak planks that let me catch the murmur of voices. One of those, weary and weak as it was, undoubtedly came from my mistress.

"I have told you, and told you before, Gabriel, I have no idea what you're talking about. Please, for the sake of old friendship, do you have a coffee, or even a tisane? Your ruffian absconded with me before my petit déjeuner, and quite frankly, I had an *exhausting* night." Her voice became louder as she spoke, and I could hear the witty, flirtatious tones I knew from Versailles taking over.

"I apologize, Catherine, for any rough treatment you received at my servant's hands. I will send for a meal shortly. But I must know."

"Gabriel," she said slowly, as if to a child, "the Marquise de Brinvilliers died. Most say by your order, if not your hand."

There was a thump and rattle, perhaps the sound of a fist on a table.

"That is a lie."

"That she died? Or by your hand?" Madame's unruffled voice sounded stronger yet.

"I did not order her killed."

"But you ordered her tortured." A touch of heat crept into her words.

"I opposed that as well." His voice was thick with emotion. "And she did not die."

Madame made no response at first, and I was left to imagine her mild, unyielding expression. Finally, she said, "Then where is she?"

"Not where she should be."

Madame gave a fulsome sigh and diverted the conversation. "Am I a captive, Gabriel? I weary of this fairy tale, and would like to go back to the inn where my retinue awaits."

"*Captive* is far too strong a word, Catherine. You are a guest of His Majesty."

"His Majesty need only send a message to my household at Versailles to reach me."

"He would rather account for your movements more closely than that. And he requests your presence at Versailles."

"In chains?"

"On your own volition would be preferable."

"Then I will be on my way. I was already heading there."

There was an awkward silence. "The road is dangerous, Madame. And my officers have leave only to protect the streets of Paris."

"I am not without defences, sir." Another pause and, I imagined, an exchange of looks. "At least give me coffee for the love of God, man. I hear there's a Turkish shop not far from here. And give me paper to write to my company."

I heard the movement of a chair, and I raced to the bottom of the staircase, Madame's kerchief clutched in one hand, my skirts bunched in the other. I fairly tumbled down the last steps and out the bottom door. As I reached the passage below, I heard the man bellow, "Girl!"

There was a clatter and splash, followed by a curse, as a woman kicked over the bucket I'd left by the door, sending water across the stone floor.

I stuck my head back through the door to the stair. "Oui, monseigneur?" I called up, in my best approximation of a Narbonnaise.

"Coffee and bread. And a pichet of wine."

"Oui, monseigneur!"

I turned to the woman and picked up the bucket. "I'll clear this up — you get the tray."

"Who are you?" asked the servant.

"His guest's maid. Where are your mops?"

She showed me to the kitchen and handed me a mop, still muttering epithets. I swabbed the floor, watching the end door in case Madame or the man Gabriel appeared. I returned the mop to the kitchen. "I'll take that up," I said, grateful that my grey wool skirt and well-travelled apron were similar enough to hers. I palmed a paring knife from the table and slid it between the coffee urn and the plate.

Tray in hand, I elbowed the door open and headed back upstairs. The upper door was ajar. I turned and pushed it open with my back, keeping my head down and surveying the room from under my cap. Madame sat at a small table, writing, and the gentleman stood facing the fireplace, his jupon lifted to warm his knees.

I brought the tray to Madame, and as I set it in front of her, I dropped the yellow pebble and the bloodstained handkerchief in her lap. Her hand closed over them and her eyes darted up to meet mine, a multitude of emotions running across her face.

"Toinette," she mouthed, her shoulders sagging — in relief, or something else? The next word her lips formed was "Orléans." Did she mean my friend, the duchess? Our enemy, the duke? Or the place itself? Out loud, she said, "Thank you, mademoiselle. You are an angel of mercy. Be so kind as to pour me a cup. Gabriel — a demitasse for you?"

I moved my body to block his view as I picked up the silver ewer, revealing the kitchen knife. Madame reached, as if for the sugar, and swept the knife into her lap, from whence I had no doubt it would find its way to her sleeve or bodice. In small retribution for the man's treatment of Madame, I decided to place the silver sugar tongs in my apron pocket.

"I've eaten," said Gabriel. To me he said, "Thank you," and nodded towards the door. "You may go."

"Wait, my friend. This girl can take my message," Madame said. "I'll gladly give her a pistole to bear the letter, and we can be on our way all the sooner."

"I'll read it first." He held out an impatient hand. He was an older man, judging by his girth and the creases in his face, but he wore his wig dark and moved with the energy of youth. He took the letter to the window to read.

The minute Gabriel's back was turned, Madame pulled the handkerchief from her lap and wrote upon it. The ink started to bleed instantly, but I could make out *8 r.SC Jeanne*. She handed it back to me and I tucked it into my pocket with the tongs. "Follow," she mouthed. This time the word was as clear as day.

With a grunt, Gabriel handed the letter to me. "Where should I take it?" I asked, keeping my gaze on Madame's face as I curtsied.

Madame reached out and took my hand. "To Antoine Fabron." My name, and Henri's surname. She gave the location of our inn and finished, "With my eternal thanks." She brought her other hand to mine, and I felt the weight of the ruby necklace slip into my grasp once more.

Before I had even crossed back over the Pont des Marchands, Henri's tall head appeared, weaving through the crowd from Mangetout's back. In front of him, less visible at their height, was the goat girl on Marteau. Luc brought up the rear, leading Babette and her cart with one hand and the prancing Habibi with the other. I waved them towards a calm space in the teeming market.

Jacques's grey form wove through the crowd in a sinuous gallop, nearly toppling me as he planted his giant forefeet on my shoulders. "Down, Jacques!" I thought I had trained him better than this in my year at la Tectume. He sat, wriggled his haunches, and let out a barely audible whine. "I am glad to see you as well, mon ami." I scruffled his head to show I wasn't truly angry. In fact, I was more glad to see all of them than I could express. "Is everything packed?" I asked Luc.

He nodded. "Except the coffee. I could find none. Where is the countess?"

"She's had plenty of coffee by now, and is likely drinking more to delay her departure for our benefit." I handed the letter to Henri, for Luc still could not read.

Henri unfolded the parchment and read out loud. "'My dear Antoine.'" He lifted his eyebrow at the masculine form of my name. "'My good friend M de la Reynie has offered me a carriage ride to Versailles to save me the trial of the roads. You know how I despise the saddle.'" We both knew Madame loved to ride. "'I shall meet you there. Do not trouble yourself by stopping at Mme LaMotte's estate. I shall do that en route. Godspeed, my friend, and farewell till we meet under His Majesty's welcoming roof.' What does that mean, not to stop at LaMotte's? Who is she?"

I pulled out the handkerchief. "She also gave me an address: rue SC — St Cyr, St Claire, St Cloud? — and mouthed the word *Orléans*. And a name, Jeanne LaM. She is asking us to go there."

"But why?" asked Luc. "She says in her letter to meet her at Versailles."

"She says she hates to ride, she addresses this to a person who does not exist, but who is Henri and me both … I think she wants us to go to this Madame LaMotte. And I think that Versailles is anything but welcoming."

"Orléans it is, then," said Henri. "How soon?"

"The carriage horses at Benavent have not been unhitched," I replied. "I warrant they are planning to leave within the hour. I think we should wait till they do, then follow at a wise distance." I turned to the girl, still sitting astride Marteau. "Down, mademoiselle." I held up my arms to assist her. "I need my horse."

"You promised me a ride on that one." She pointed at Habibi.

"I promised you could sit on him." I picked her up by the waist and transferred her to the restive stallion. Habibi fidgeted under her, his hind hooves tapping the cobbles nervously. Without taking my hand from the rein, I reached into my purse for the three sols I'd promised her. "That is for bringing my friends to me. Now, here is a souvenir from today." I retrieved the stolen sugar tongs from my apron and handed them to her. "Do not sell it today, or even this year. Keep it safe, and if you ever find yourself needing to leave your home for any reason, sell it then, for as high a price as you can, and send a message to Antoinette Berger in the service of the Countess of Athlone at Versailles. You will receive welcome there. Can you repeat that back to me?"

She did, but as she recited the words, the joyous glint in her eyes dulled and faded. I noticed the yellow hue of a faded bruise across one cheek, a poorly healed scar on her chin, and a fresher purple mark, the size of man's thumb, showing at the edge of her too-short sleeve. I touched her face, and she flinched—from habit, it seemed. "Is now the time you need to leave, ma petite?"

She bit her lip, and gave the faintest of nods.

"Is there anything you need from your home?"

The tiny nod turned to a shake.

"What about your family? Your mama?"

"I have no mother. My sisters have married and left home."

I touched the bruise on her arm. "Is this from a goat?"

She shook her head.

"Your papa? Your brother?"

I couldn't tell which one the nod referred to, but it didn't matter.

"What is your name, child?"

"Anne Chevrier."

I laughed to myself. Of course it was.

"Toinette," warned Henri, "you can't take in every stray that looks at you with large eyes."

Jacques whined in protest, and Luc studied Babette's harness.

"You took me in," I said. "Or perhaps it was the other way around."

"She will slow us down."

"Nonsense. She's no slower than Luc with poor Babette. And she's a better rider." I turned back to her. "Anne," I said, "would you rather come with us?"

The light in her eyes bloomed again, and she took up Habibi's reins.

I shook my head and picked her up by the waist once more, putting her back on Marteau. "You're not that good a rider yet, ma petite."

Neither was I, to be honest, but I held my breath and made a brave show as I put my foot in Habibi's stirrup. The stallion started forward before I had settled in the saddle, and I pulled too hard on his delicate mouth in my quick urge to stop him. He protested with a half rear and spun a quarter turn on his haunches. It took all my minimal skill to stay on his back, but as I loosened the rein, he settled. Heart in mouth, I took up the right stirrup and smiled with false courage.

"Tiens," I said, hoping my voice sounded bolder than I felt. "Lead us to your home, so we may leave a message for your father."

§

Find out what happens in the next instalment of The Shepherdess *in* Pulp Literature *Issue 46, Spring 2025.*

Now Available!

Allaigna's Song
Overture
AMAZON #1 BESTSELLER
JM Landels
Allaigna's Song
Aria
JM Landels
Allaigna's Song
Chorale
JM Landels
The magical conclusion to the must-read epic trilogy
the adventures of Allaigna sing
simply a joy to read
keeps you turning pages from beginning to end
an immensely satisfying epic
PULPLITERATURE.COM/ALLAIGNAS-SONG/

THE ARTISTS

Bronwyn Schuster
Cover artist, Ceren of the Surf
Bronwyn (she/they) is a Canadian painter and illustrator. Born to a family of artists in the mountains of Alberta and raised in the grasslands of Saskatchewan, Bronwyn furthered their studies at the Swedish Academy of Realist Art, and now resides on Denman Island with her partner and two cats.

Bronwyn explores many mediums, including oil, gouache, watercolour, and coloured pencil to create drawings, paintings, and murals that weave nature and folklore together. Through art making, the artist seeks to find the magic in the mundane and the ordinary in the fantastic.

Their painting *Space Cat,* which can be found on *Pulp Literature* Issue 33, Winter 2022, remains one of our most popular covers to date. *Ceren of the Surf* is part of her series Knights of the Drowned Table. You can see the full painting, along with many other stunning works by Bronwyn Schuster, at www.nywn.art.

Gabriel Craven and Mikayla Fawcett
Creators, 'Bad Backup'
'Bad Backup' is a short story from *Final Restoration,* Gabriel and Mikayla's series about the zombie-fighting blue-collar workers at a restoration company of the same name. It started in 2016 as a series of strips poking fun at zombie apocalypse escapism

fantasies where the characters break out of their mundane lives and become post-apocalyptic badasses. What if zombies attacked, and, instead of the full societal reset, most of us went back to business as usual? Drawing from working experience in the restoration industry, the creators felt that zombies made a natural addition to the roster of job site hazards. There's a life-threatening pandemic out there, and you've still got to make rent somehow. Absurd? Sure. But what can you do?

For more post-apocalyptic tales of working stiffs in the zombie apocalypse, see 'High Reward' in *Pulp Literature* Issue 42, Spring 2024, and 'Afloat' in *Pulp Literature* Issue 17, Winter 2018.

Mel Anastasiou
In-house illustrator
Mel Anastasiou loves drawing for *Pulp Literature* because she loves the stories she illustrates. She draws in black and white, working from imagination and inspired by details from Renaissance compositions. You can find illustrations, writing tips, and news about her books and novellas at melanastasiou. wordpress.com, and see more of her artwork on Facebook at Bird and Branch Artwork

HALL OF FAME

These are the heroes — the Patrons and Pulp Literati whose monthly support helped bring you this issue. Please lift your glasses and give them a rousing cheer!

The Brewers
Dana Tye Rally

The Innkeepers
Abigail Bruce
Andrea Kepple
David Jensen
Ev Bishop
Gillian Gardiner
Kevin Harris
Lorna Ens
Mark Francis
Richard Ohnemus
Robin McGillveray
Susan Jackson
Kevin S Moul

The Cicerones
Jennifer Sommersby
Roger & Anne Anastasiou
Zoë Ricard

The Bartenders
Alana Krider
Andrea Kirkham
Anna Belkine
April DC
Benjamin Johnson
Bjarne Hansen
Brighton Hugg

Bryan Moose
Chris Olee
Dave Wayne
Deepthi Atukorala
Devan Erno
Ernst Pulido
Evelyn Ann
Finnian Burnett
Fran Scannell
James Carlino
Jennifer Getsinger
Jillian Shoichet
John Olley
K Anastasiou
Katherine Derbyshire
Katriona Greenmoor
kc dyer
KT Wagner
Leny Wagner
Lin & John Richardson
Margaret Elliott
Margot Landels
Margot Spronk
Maureen Cooke
Megan Shaw
Michelle Balfour
Mike Sylvester
Peter Halasz
Rapscallion
Richard Gropp

Ron Graves
Scott F Gray
Scott Carrothers
Shannon Saunders
Star
Suzanne Philip
Venasa Simpson

The Regulars
Adam Fout
Akemi Art
Andy W
BC
Catherine Levinson
Charity Tahmaseb
David Perlmutter
James Gotaas
Jenny Blackford
Marilyn Holt
Marta Salek
Meredith Frazier
Paul Anguiano
Rhea Rose
Rina Piccolo
Sonia Brock
Vera
Emmy Bee
JS Andrew
Michelle Robinson

If you would like to join the ranks of these worthies, you can become a patron on Patreon at patreon.com/pulplit or join the Pulp Literati through our website at pulpliterature.com/join-pulp-literati/.

Do you have a **story to tell?**
We can help!

Dreamers is dedicated to heartfelt writing. Visit our site for:

- Therapeutic Writing
- Poems & Stories
- Content Marketing
- Creative Nonfiction
- Writing Workshops
- Contests & Anthologies
- Residencies & Retreats
- ...and so much more!

www.DreamersWriting.com

In search of a writing community?

Join today!

The Federation of BC Writers is here for you!

- ☑ Workshops/ Webinars
- ☑ Contests
- ☑ Readings
- ☑ Articles

- ☑ Networking
- ☑ Discount Membership for for Students and Seniors

- ☑ Digital Writing Circles
- ☑ Find Inspiration & more!

bcwriters.ca/Join

Keep it weird. Subscribe today!

MARKETPLACE

Books

Advent *by Michael Kamakana* • We thought we knew what the aliens wanted. Think again. • pulpliterature.com/advent

Allaigna's Song: Chorale *by JM Landels* The long-awaited conclusion to the bestselling *Allaigna's Song* trilogy. • pulpliterature.com/allaignas-song

The Extra: A Monument Studios Mystery *by Mel Anastasiou* • Extra Frankie Ray gets her big break on the Silver Screen, until murder steals the scene. • pulpliterature.com/the-extra

The Labours of Mrs Stella Ryman: Further Fairmount Mysteries *by Mel Anastasiou* • Trapped in a down-at-the-heels care home. You'd be cranky too. • pulpliterature.com/stella-ryman-and-the-fairmount-manor-mysteries

What the Wind Brings *by Matthew Hughes* • Winner of the 2020 Endeavour Award • pulpliterature.com/product-category/novels/matthew-hughes

The Writer's Boon Companion *by Mel Anastasiou* • Thirty Days Towards an Extraordinary Volume • pulpliterature.com/subscribe/the-bookstore

Bookstores

Russell Books • 100-747 Fort St, Victoria, BC • russellbooks.com

Western Sky Books • 2132-2850 Shaughnessy St, Port Coquitlam, BC V3C6K5 • 604-461-5602 • store.westernskybooks.com

White Dwarf / Dead Write Books • 3715 10th Ave W, Vancouver, BC V6R 2G5 • 604-228-8223 whitedwarf@deadwrite.com

Conferences & Events

Surrey International Writers' Conference 24-27 October 2024 • siwc.ca

When Words Collide • August 2025 Calgary, AB • whenwordscollide.org

Wine Country Writers' Festival • Sep 2025 winecountrywriters-festival.ca

Printing & Publishing

First Choice Books/Victoria Bindery Book printing & binding • graphic design • eBooks • marketing materials 1-800-957-0561 • firstchoicebooks.ca

Writing Resources

Dreamers Creative Writing • Workshops, residencies, contests & more! • www.dreamerswriting.com

Federation of BC Writers • Workshops • contests • networking & more! www.bcwriters.ca/join-us

MAGAZINES

Amazing Stories · Back in print! amazingstories.com

Arc Poetry Magazine · Poetry, essays, interviews, reviews · arcpoetry.ca

The Digest Enthusiast · Digests past & present plus new genre fiction larquepress.com

EVENT Magazine · Poetry & prose eventmagazine.ca

Geist · Ideas + Culture · Made in Canada · geist.com

Malahat Review · Poetry, fiction, creative non-fiction · www.malahatreview.ca

Mystery Weekly Magazine · The cutting edge of short mystery fiction www.mysteryweekly.com

Neo-opsis · Canadian magazine of science fiction based in Victoria, BC · neo-opsis.ca

OnSpec · The Canadian magazine of the fantastic · onspecmag.wordpress.com

Polar Borealis · Paying market for new Canadian SF&F writers & artists · polarborealis.ca

Room Magazine · Literature, Art & Feminism since 1975 · roommagazine.com

PULP Literature

The Bumblebee
Flash Fiction Contest
Deadline: 15 February
Prize $300

The Magpie Award for Poetry
Deadline: 15 April
Prize $500

The Hummingbird Flash Fiction Prize
Deadline: 15 June
Prize $300

The Raven Short Story Contest
Deadline: 15 October
Prize $300

The Kingfisher Poetry Prize
Deadline: 15 November
Prize $300

Enter today:
pulpliterature.com/contests

CONTESTS

Pulp Literature runs six annual contests for poetry, flash fiction, short stories, and novel first pages. For contest guidelines, prizes, and entry fees, see pulpliterature.com/contests.

The Kingfisher Poetry Prize
Contest opens: 1 October 2024
Deadline: 15 November 2024
Winner notified: 15 December 2024
Winner published: Issue 46, Spring 2025
Prize: $300

The Bumblebee Flash Fiction Contest
Contest opens: 1 January 2025
Deadline: 15 February 2025
Winner notified: 15 March 2025
Winner published: Issue 47, Summer 2025
Prize: $300

The Magpie Award for Poetry
Contest opens: 1 March 2025
Deadline: 15 April 2025
Winner notified: 15 May 2025
Winner published: Issue 48, Autumn 2025
Prize: $500

The Hummingbird Flash Fiction Prize

Contest opens: 1 May 2025
Deadline: 15 June 2025
Winner notified: 15 July 2025
Winner published: Issue 49, Winter 2026
Prize: $300

The First Page Cage

Contest opens: 1 August 2025
Deadline: 15 September 2025
Winner notified: 15 October 2025
Quarter-finalists published online: Autumn 2025
Prize: $300

The Raven Short Story Contest

Contest opens: 1 September 2025
Deadline: 15 October 2025
Winner notified: 15 November 2025
Winner published: Issue 50, Spring 2026
Prize: $300

EVENT

36th ANNUAL NON-FICTION CONTEST

INCREASED CASH PRIZES
$1,500 • $1,000 • $500

OCTOBER 15

Non-Fiction Contest winners feature in every volume since 1989 and have received recognition from the Canadian Magazine Awards, National Magazine Awards and Best Canadian Essays. All entries considered for publication. Entry fee of $34.95 includes a one-year subscription. We encourage writers from diverse backgrounds and experience levels to submit their work.

eventmagazine.ca

The **Digest Enthusiast**

Book Sixteen C
September 2023

A Peek at
Jeanne
Carmen's
Magazine
Bibliography

Exploring
the Unknown,
Fantastic,
Handi-Books,
Health
Knowledge,
Jonah Hex,
Manhunt,

Startling Mystery Stories, and more.

MATTHEW HUGHES
What the Wind Brings

Allaigna's Song
Overture
AMAZON #1 BESTSELLER
J M Landels

PULP Literature
JTF King
Susan Pieters
Kathryn Yelinek
Leo X Robertson
Heather Christle
David Ly
Robert Silverberg
'The Pope of the Chimps'

MICHAEL KAMAKANA
ADVENT
WE THOUGHT WE KNEW WHAT THEY WANTED
WE WERE WRONG

Become a Patron of Pulp Literature

By supporting *Pulp Literature* on Patreon with $2 or more per month, you will be laying the foundation for a secure future for the magazine, as well as ensuring that you never miss an issue! Your subscription includes four big issues of short stories, novellas, poetry, comics, and novel excerpts, delivered to your door or electronic mailbox each year. **Find us at patreon.com/pulplit**

If you prefer to subscribe through our website, go to pulpliterature.com/subscribe.

Or you can send a cheque with the form below to
Subscriptions, Pulp Literature Press, 21955 16 Ave, Langley BC, V2Z 1K5, Canada

☐ **Send me 2 years (8 issues) at the special rate of $110** (save $34)*
☐ **Send me 1 year (4 issues) for $60** (save $12)*
☐ **Send me 2 years of digital issues for $35** (save $12.92)
☐ **Send me 1 year of digital issues for $20** (save $3.96)

Name: ____

Address: ____

City: ________________________________ Prov. / State: _________

Postal code: ______________ Country: __________________

Email: ____

☐ Payment enclosed
☐ Bill me
☐ New
☐ Renewal

Make cheques payable in Canadian funds to Pulp Literature Press. Include email address for digital editions and Paypal billing, or subscribe at www.pulpliterature.com/subscribe.

*for postage outside Canada add $20 per year in North America or $32 per year overseas.

9 781988 865676